Aftermath of an Addiction

By Sandra Shrewsbury

Aftermath of an Addiction
Sandra Shrewsbury

The following story contains strong situations. The following story is intended for adult audiences only. Parental discretion is advised.

Cover design by No Cover Designs
https://www.facebook.com/nocoverdesigns

Edited by Big Bang Book Services

Part 1

Susan's Story

Chapter One

Destroy our lives once more!

The words were enough to send a cold chill of terror down my spine. Our lives had been irrevocably destroyed; we would never see our angels again. Tears pricked my eyes, but I forced them back and shook my head. No. I never thought this day would come. The day when justice would not prevail, the day my daughter would destroy our lives once more. How did I tell them that she was fighting me for full custody of them? "Dammit," I muttered, frustration beginning to peak. The real question was would she win? I had to look out for their best interests. And I was determined to do whatever it took to make sure my grandchildren were happy, to keep them safe. She could not win this battle. I didn't know why she bothered; she hadn't shown any concern over the children for years now. My mind was racing and plagued by the fear of something terrible happening to them if she did get them back.

I had to figure out a plan to keep her from getting them back. I knew she was still using drugs, but proving it was going to be harder. She always had a way of passing her drug screens and I didn't have a clue as to how. The social worker said she had been clean for over a year, but she called me about a month ago and could hardly speak without slurring her words. I only had a month until the court date so I would have to work fast.

I would need all the help I could get to prove she was unfit to take care of these children. I had to imagine the worst-case scenario: she wins the battle and she destroys their precious lives. I could not let that happen and I would not let that happen. I had had Kelly and Amy for five years now. Kelly just turned seven last month and Amy was five years old now. They had grown into beautiful young ladies and they were happy and content with their lives. No judge in their right mind would let her have them back, but I couldn't take that chance. Something had to be done.

There was a knock on the door. *Who could that be?*

"Hi Jackie," I greeted her. "I didn't think you'd be coming for a visit this weekend."

Jackie had moved away two years ago to take care of her sick sister, Kathy. She still found time to visit on the weekends sometimes. It seemed she always knew when I needed her the most. We went into the kitchen, our favorite place to chat and drink coffee. I, unfortunately, knew from experience that anything I said would simply make matters worse and put more pressure on an already overwhelmed Jackie. So I started out by asking her how her sister was doing. She was doing a lot better and Jackie was talking about coming back home. I was so delighted to hear that she was coming home. I needed her support through this mess. I didn't know how to tell her about Tina fighting me for custody of Kelly and Amy, So I excused myself for a minute. I walked into the living room and stood there thinking of how she was going to take the news. I could not put it off any longer; I had to go into the kitchen. I had to tell her, because she loved those two like they were her own grandchildren.

I knew it would be hard on her, but I also knew how it would go. We would rehash the days that Tina turned our world upside down and settle on a plan of attack for the next day.

As I went back into the kitchen, Jackie looked at me and said, "Ok come out with it. I know something is wrong." I sighed. She always knew; I guess that was why we were so close. I started from the beginning and told her everything. She sat and listened and did not say a word until I had finished. I could see the tears forming in her eyes and I felt the sadness in her heart. My emotions were running on overdrive and I started to cry with her. "We cannot let this happen, Susan," Jackie said. "We must come up with a plan to stop her. Is she still doing drugs?"

"She told the social workers that she has been clean for over a year now, but I talked to her last month and she was messed up then. She asked me if she could come home and I told her no. She hung up on me and hasn't called since." I looked up at the clock on the wall. "The girls will be home soon and I don't want them to know about this yet, so let's start a plan tomorrow when they leave for school. I don't want them upset until we know for sure what will happen."

Jackie agreed.

The night couldn't have been any longer and frustrating. I went through my normal routine and acted like nothing was wrong. Gratefully, I climbed into the shower. The tepid water washed away most of the dirt and grit. However, while toweling myself dry, the sweat began to reform. The heat was unbearable this year. Looking out my window before I crawled into bed, I was relieved to see that the living room light was on at Jackie's house. Just knowing she was back was so much comfort to me. Sleep would not come and all I could do was think about what we were going to do to save my grandchildren. I knew Tina was still doing drugs and I did not want those children to go through that. I had to find out if she really was clean or not. I had to have proof. I would fight her to the bitter end if I have to.

Lying on my bed, I propped my tired head up against the headboard.

***

I must have instantly fallen asleep as I awoke with a startle. I listened intently, trying to discover what had awakened me. Far away I heard a muffled sound. Realization dawned, and I knew what was happening. It was the laughter of children. Kelly and Amy were playing in their room.

I hurried up and got dressed so I could check on the girls and get them ready for school. Probably a good idea with them girls. They were more daring than I was at their age. They thought of too many things to try.

They were dare devils and would try anything. As I walked up to their door, I could hear their laughter and my heart melted. I felt satisfaction in seeing my grandchildren happy. I called for them to follow me to the kitchen so they could eat before heading out to school.

While replenishing the milk into their glasses, I watched the girls and thought about how cute they looked. They were seated on benches next to their table. Blond-haired Amy had blue eyes while brown-haired Kelly had brown eyes. They looked like sisters, but definitely were not the same. Their personalities were totally different from each other's. Amy was the shy one and Kelly was very outspoken. I loved them both the same, though.

They finished their breakfast and got their coats on. I hugged each one and didn't want to let go, but Kelly yelled, "Grandma, we are going to be late for the bus."

I said my goodbyes and they ran out the door to the bus stop. A thought came to my mind. *What if I never get to do this again?* What would I do if I lost them? The tears started to roll down my cheeks. I took in a huge breath and calmed myself so I would be level headed when Jackie got there. I knew that with Jackie's help we would find something out that would keep the judge from giving her the girls.

I sat and waited on Jackie to arrive. I was on my second cup of coffee when there was a knock at the door. Jackie followed me into the kitchen and I made

11

her some coffee. "I never expected this to happen," Jackie said.

"I didn't either. We have to find a way to stop it from happening." We sat and talked about how we could catch her buying drugs and taking photos of it. We could use it in court. First, we would have to find out where she was living and then follow her.

This was going to be hard, but I could make a few phone calls to find out where she lived. I grinned. "I guess I can't talk you into going with me to follow her. I don't want to do this alone."

"You don't even have to ask; I will be right there with you."

I spent most of the afternoon calling all her old friends and nothing not one led to where she was living. I had one more to call and I hoped she knew where Tina lived. It was Tina's best friend, Alice Baker. She always knew how to find Tina. I dialed the number and it rang forever until, finally, a young woman's voice was on the other end.

"This is Tina Green's mother. Do you know where she is living now, Alice? I really must get in contact with her."

"Yes....I know the address," Alice replied.

"Thank you so much for your help, Alice!"

I wrote the address down and we said our goodbyes.

I looked at Jackie and then took a long deep breath and exhaled heavily, hoping to expel the last decade of pain into the air. We had our start, and it was now time to plan what to do next. Jackie and I planned everything that afternoon. We were going to start following her tomorrow after the girls went to school. I felt like I was going crazy. What was I doing following my own daughter? I just had to make sure that the girls would be okay.

***

Jackie left before the girls got home from school. Amy was the first to come running through the door. She was waving her arms at me and I waved back with both arms, laughing at her antics, thinking how she had that same free-spirited gene as her mother. I glanced at the anxious faces of the girls. I knew they were waiting on me to get their after school snacks ready. I had been so busy planning everything today that I had forgot to make them ahead of time.

This was our time to catch up on what happened at school. As they ate their snacks they would tell me how their day went. This was my favorite time of the day. Kelly would always talk about her teacher, Mrs. Hall. She loved her teacher this year. Amy always talked about what they did in class. She loved to draw.

My phone vibrated. A text from Jackie read, **I have more info. Call me when you get a chance.** *Awesome*, I thought. I was anxious to see if my feelings were true about her doing drugs still. I really was hoping that I was wrong and she had cleaned herself up. A part of me knew better, though. The girls went upstairs to play and I started dinner for us. I wanted to get everything done early so I could get some sleep before our big journey tomorrow. Kelly came in to help set the table as she always did.

"Sweetie, would you get a cup of punch for your sister and you?"

She was eager to help; I think it made her feel special. Dinner was full of conversation as always and then we watched a movie together.

I was so tired by the time bedtime came that I fell asleep and forgot to call Jackie about what she found out.

A cold feeling ran up my spine and a chill settled on my arms. I realized I was holding Tina in my arms and she was not breathing. I could feel the tears coming from my eyes. I wondered for a moment if I'd caused it with my mean thoughts about her. I stared at her, wanting to take back every bad thought I'd ever had.

"How can you be dead?" I whispered. She didn't look like Tina, but I recognized her. Then my mind clicked into place and I realized, "Oh my god! It's Kelly."

I jumped out of bed, sweating like crazy. It was a dream. It felt so real; I could still feel her in my arms.

I could not go back to sleep right away. I went to the bathroom to wash my face and calm down. I wished this were over with. I didn't know how much more strength I had left in me.

Chapter Two

The hunt for the truth begins!

The next morning, I was woken by the sound of the ringing telephone. I didn't get to it in time, but I knew it had to be Jackie. She was probably making sure I was awake. I walked toward my bedroom window and I could smell the flowers growing outside, delighting my senses and waking me up. It was a beautiful morning. The sun had a bright glow to it, which made everything shine. The trees seemed to glisten and the clouds were white wisps among the light blue sky. Our world was such a beautiful place. My heart felt at peace while staring out at the gorgeous sky.

Then reality hit like a slap in the face. I had to get the girls ready for school so Jackie and I could follow Tina today.

***

Jackie had come over right after the girls had left for school. I had a cup of coffee waiting on her and when she walked inside she smiled gratefully. We hurried and drank our coffee and then we were on our way.

Exhilarating? Yes. Insane? Absolutely! I felt like a private investigator, or like a spy on a mission. Jackie walked ahead of me down the driveway. Her dark brown hair blanketed her shoulders, falling halfway down her back. You could see spots of grey shimmering in the rays of light.

As we were getting into the car, Jackie looked over at me and said, "Susan, this is the craziest thing we have ever done."

"Probably." I paused. "No, I have to say, most definitely!"

***

We approached the home—the home where my Tina spent most of her time. It was a small blue house with white shutters. It seemed to be very nice from the outside. I was impatient to get out of there. The hours dragged by. I didn't think we would ever see Tina come out of her house. I got so bored I took my hair out of the ponytail, messed it up a little, and combed it with my fingers. My hair spilled down my back in gentle waves. In the sunlight, the auburn highlights from the sun danced with each curl. I should wear my hair down more often.

Jackie hit me with her elbow. "Susan there she is."

I froze. I hadn't seen Tina in over five years. She was very thin and looked pale. A tear came to my eye as I remembered the old daughter I once had known. We stayed far back so she wouldn't spot us. She walked forever it seemed. She stopped at a little market on the corner. Jackie and I watched her come out with a pack of cigarettes. She headed back in the same direction as she came. This was a wasted trip; she went straight back to the little house.

"We will try again tomorrow, Susan," Jackie said.

"Is this going to work, Jackie?" I asked.

"Yes; it is just going to take time."

It was almost three o'clock when we returned home. Almost time for the girls to get home from school. Jackie came in with me so she could spend some time with the girls before they had to go to bed.

Even with our busy schedules, we made sure to make time for each other—whether it was cooking a meal together, going to the movies, or just hanging around the house and laughing. I believe it had become our ritual. My business had been booming and I was busy most days of the week. So I was very glad I had this vacation time I could take. I missed being a nurse, but I didn't miss the long hours. After I got the girls, I realized that I couldn't work all those long hours anymore. So I opened up a small bakery in town. I always loved to bake. I set my own hours and I had plenty of time to spend with the girls. Donnie continued to run the phone at the shop and he took the orders and Liz did the baking when I was not there. It all worked out great. I hired Donnie and Liz right after I opened the bakery. They were married and just starting their lives together. They were in need of a job and I was in need of

17

employees. They were both in their early twenties. They both seemed very reasonable and dependable. After their interview, I hired them both on the spot. They lived on my street so it was easy to find out what kind of people they were. All I had to do was visit the local gossip group for about five minutes and I found out all I needed to know.

I must have gotten lost in a few moments of lonely daydreams, because when I looked over Jackie and the girls were looking at me strangely. I couldn't help but laugh at all of them. Jackie went home and I got the girls ready for bed. I took a long hot bath to try and relax. I fell asleep in the tub. The dream was the same every time. Fog covered my eyes, but I could hear the people around me crying. I put my hands out, trying to reach out to them. No one took my hand. Then I was holding Kelly in my arms again. I had a terrible feeling it was my fault.

"Wake up, Susan." I knew the soft voice. It was Kelly who whispered to me.

I woke, startled, feeling my own embrace and the beads of sweat that soaked me. I looked around, dazed, expecting to see someone. I had been certain a voice had woken me. I got out and dried myself, dressed, and went to my bed. The enveloping darkness was a warm comfort inside my bed. I fell back to sleep and dreamt of her again. In the new dream, I floated, staring at her with Tina and Amy. I was unable to float down to touch them or move at all. I floated in limbo, watching them. I felt so helpless and lost. My chest felt as though it ripped into a million tiny shards.

I knew hope was taken from my world. At that moment, I didn't know just how large of a piece it was. Tina had the girls and I was all alone. I was devoid of every feeling. I knew if I acknowledged one pain, I would have to face the others. This was so real. Was it a dream or was I really losing them forever? Then the dream took a crazy turn. I was holding my daughter in my arms. My heart beat out of my chest, but I closed my eyes and let the world stop. I needed to feel her. Even if it was for a moment, she was there. I was holding my little girl once again. I didn't want this to end.

***

The breakfast table the next morning felt grim, as I contemplated my dreams. As usual, I remembered very little. That morning seemed to feel worse than most days. I had been certain that I had started to gain a little hope, but the bad dreams hadn't helped.

"Earth to Susan," Jackie said. Kelly had let her in. I looked up from my lost gaze to see my best friend staring at me. I knew Jackie was worried about me, but she wasn't one to be pointing fingers. She looked so worried herself. I knew she had not slept because of the dark circles under her eyes. It was rare for her to make eye contact with other people, except me. Being her best friend and the only person able to beat her in cards, earned me at least a bit of eye contact. "You look like shit today, Susan."

She was the only person who could be mean to me and make a smile come across my face. "I look beautiful." I tried to be serious.

She shook her head, as she looked me straight in the eyes. "No, you don't and you're starting to look like a zombie."

I shook my head. "I'm not a morning person, okay?"

Her face was red as she ranted. "You need sleep; you have these girls to take care of."

On that day, in that moment, I felt like giving up. Normally, I would have ignored it, but I was so exhausted. I had to snap out of this state of mind. "There, just for you, Jackie." I pushed back my pain and smiled. Jackie smiled back at me. I couldn't help but smile at Jackie with her funny sarcastic ways, which cheered me up, even when I resisted. I stood up, feeling blood rushing back into my legs with painful pins and needles. "I Love you, Jackie. You win, okay?" I made everyone breakfast and got the girls off to school.

***

We were on our way back to Tina's house. I had to confess, the idea of being at Tina's house, did make my heart ache. Jackie and I were contemplating the possibility of Tina getting the children back. When she came out the door and walked up the road again, I nodded and ignored the sick feeling in my stomach. We stayed back far enough to where she couldn't see us but we could see her. I was secretly wishing she was just going to the store again, but one side of me was reasonable and the other was realistic. My heart ached again. I couldn't help but worry. If she was not doing drugs anymore, I would lose the girls. And if she was and I couldn't prove it, the girls and I both lose. I couldn't get over how horridly thin she looked.

She stopped at a house and went inside. "Oh my God—she went in that house! I will be right back," I said. Tina was in and out before I could register what had happened. Without warning, Jackie grabbed me and pulled me behind a car. "Did she see us?"

"I don't think so."

I didn't even want to think about the fact that we almost got caught because of me reacting too fast. Jackie grabbed my arm and dragged me to the car.

"You want to catch her, don't you, Susan? You need to start thinking before you react."

I nodded, trying to pacify her as she ranted. Jackie, who always seemed to be right, drove off to see if she could find her.

"I hope we can find her again," I said.

"Yeah, well, don't get your hopes up," Jackie replied.

Feeling like an idiot, I just sat there in silence. Deep in thought about Tina, I didn't even realize Jackie had found her again. She tried not to let her get too far ahead of us. Her outdated fur jacket made it easy to keep her in our sights. She turned down a dark alley. I grimaced, and wondered if, perhaps, she was looking for her next fix.

She rounded the corner, and we stayed across the street from her, and so she couldn't see us. I wondered if Jackie was going to permit me to follow her. Eager to follow her, I shivered in anticipation. "Stay where you are." Her voice never wavered, but I could sense the anger coming off her. She assessed the alley and the danger before telling me to follow. "Really, who would go into a place like this? This alley is filthy with trash and God only knows what else." Closer. I felt the air suck from my body as I stood under the broken streetlight in the alley, which clearly the city's maintenance had forgotten. I gulped, pushing down my feelings. I felt frozen in panic, but also desperate to see what she was doing. I looked at her and frowned in disbelief, as I drew close enough to fully recognize that she was buying drugs.

I could see the raw emotion on her face. My lower lip trembled, followed by my entire body. I took a step back. I remembered every second of her childhood in those few seconds. Only those little moments could sooth me right now. My fear of losing her again, filled the air with my screams. I felt the tears rolling as I shouted her name. She ran to the end of the alley, desperate to get away. I ran after her as fast as I could.

"Stop!" a man's voice echoed through the alley. I didn't stop; I had to catch her. I felt the tears rolling as she listened to me shout her name, but she never stopped. My screams filled the air. "TINA!"

I needed a moment to recognize, not only where I was, but also how to get back to where Jackie was without that man seeing me. My eyes darted to the right. The face staring at me took me by surprise and I started swinging my fist.

"What the hell are you doing?" Jackie yelled.

I walked to the far side of the alley, where I sat down on a cinderblock laying up against the brick wall. Tears threatened to spring from my eyes, but I looked at Jackie and said, "I lost her all over again."

For some reason, I couldn't cry; the tears would not fall. Even with all the pain I was feeling in my heart. When Jackie looked at me, I saw an apologetic look I had never seen on her face.

"I am so sorry, Susan."

We made our way back to the car and I got in the car, slamming the door. Jackie never spoke the whole way home. She was angry and it was better for my head if she didn't talk.

Chapter Three

The Phone Call

Morning came too soon for me. I knew Jackie would be over after the girls left to ask me what happened. We didn't speak last night at all. She went home as soon as we got to my house. I knew she was mad, but not as mad as I was at myself. I don't know why I screamed out her name. I should have just got the pictures and left. It was like I was trying to save her all over again. I had to get it off my mind for now, so I started getting the girls ready for school.

Kelly and Amy loved school. They were always dressed and ready to go before I had a chance to help them. They would pick out their outfits the night before and lay them out. Kelly was picky about what she wore, but Amy didn't care. I walked the girls to the door and said our goodbyes with hugs and kisses as we did every morning.

I went into the kitchen to have a cup of coffee and wait on Jackie to arrive. I just hoped she wasn't still mad and I could make her understand why I did what I did.

It was only a few minutes before there was a knock at the door. I yelled for her to come in because I knew it was her. I could hear the creaking of the door as it opened and her footsteps coming down the hallway. I looked up as she entered the kitchen to see the expression on her face. As soon as I saw it, I knew she was still upset with me.

"What the hell did you do that for?" Jackie said. I didn't know that she knew I had screamed Tina's name when I was in the alley, but she knew. I tried to explain to Jackie why I did what I did. There was a tugging in my heart, a sense of loss and pain, as if I was losing her all over again. All my life I had battled to keep my children safe and that instinct kicked in at the wrong moment.

There were a number of sensible explanations for my actions. I just couldn't think of them at this moment. This was the first time I'd ever felt nervous around Jackie. Damn, I wished she understood how I felt. Not that it was her fault, of course. If you have never been a mother, you could hardly be blamed for your ignorance. Jackie just stared at me for a few moments longer, and then finally smiled at me. Forcing her tense muscles to relax, she stepped toward me and gave me a hug. I sagged in relief then offered her some coffee. Feeling more at ease, we finished our coffee and decided to try again. Tina didn't know that we knew where she lived so we could still follow her. I was glad in a way that she did run and I didn't get a chance to talk to her. I would have blurted everything out about us knowing where she lived.

As we were getting ready to leave, the phone rang. My heart began to pound as a sense of danger welled within me. It was Tina on the other end. Her voice filled with rage, she asked me why I was in that alley and why was I following her? I told her that I was going to a shop down that way when I saw her go into the alley and I followed to talk to her. When my heart finally quit pounding, I asked her why she was in the alley. I wanted to hear what she had to say.

Not wanting to deal with me, she just yelled, "STOP FOLLOWING ME!" And she hung up.

I looked at Jackie and tears fell from my eyes. Jackie hugged me and told me everything would be alright. I really wanted to believe her.

We decided to give it a day to let things calm down. That way Tina would think it was okay to leave her house again. Jackie started preparations for more coffee, putting water in the pot. Once the coffee was done, she poured it into our cups and leaned her hip against the kitchen counter so she could look out the window. It had been sunny when she'd set out an hour ago, but now large clouds raced across the sky while thunder rumbled loudly in the distance. Everything was still except for the branches swaying on the trees. A bright flash of lightning followed by a loud crack of thunder made her jump back away from the window.

She hurried across the kitchen to the table with our coffee in her hands. Jackie never liked a storm; it always terrified her. As for me, envisioning a cup of coffee and curling up in a chair to read while the storm blew over was a wonderful thing to do. I had always loved a good storm. Jackie leaned against the wooden surface, paralyzed with fear as the sound of thunder struck again.

"Damn it, I hate storms," she said.

I wanted to laugh at her, but I knew how terrified she really was of a storm, so I just told her it would be alright. Rain was hitting the window pane while thunder rumbled overhead, but it appeared the storm would quickly pass.

I was in deep thought when Jackie shook my arm. "I'm sorry, Jackie, what did you say?"

"I was asking if you had any ideas on how we should handle following Tina tomorrow." At that time, I had no idea of what to do next. All I knew was that we had to catch her in the act and get that picture. I could not go into that courtroom empty handed. I had to get proof she was still doing drugs. My grandchildren's lives depended on it. I asked Jackie how she got so good at following people. "I think I've spent too much time watching mystery flicks. And I've spent too much time reading Sherlock Holmes novels." She laughed.

"I don't know, Jackie, it seems to have come in handy," I replied.

***

As we continued to spend the day together, Jackie asked me how Fay and John were doing. Fay worked in a legitimate law office during school holidays; mainly helping with little stuff like filing and making coffee. Jonathan, as he prefers to be called while he lives on campus, spends weekends and school holidays with his new girlfriend. They called, but I really didn't get to see much of them anymore. They were very privileged to attend one of the best schools in California. They appeared to be very happy. There was a bond between Fay and John that was airtight, not just because of their childhoods; it went much deeper than that. I think a lot of it had to do with what we went through with Tina. They talked and saw each other daily. I was so glad they both applied for the same college, even though Fay was a year and a half older than John.

After we had chatted about the kids for a bit, Jackie and I got on the subject of books. Books are my true lovers—I'd taken far more of them to bed than I have men. And I'd been disappointed less often, too. I plowed through at least a dozen books in the past six months. One that really stuck in my head was 'Hired for Christmas' by *Genevieve Scholl*. She was an indie author on the Internet. I was telling Jackie about the book and told her she had to read it. My love life really sucked at the moment so my book boyfriends had made up for the loss. Any time Jackie and I talked about books, it seemed like time would fly by. It was almost time for the girls to get home when I realized we had been sitting there all day talking about our favorite books.

"They're here," Jackie cheered as she loved spending time with the girls. They came running in the kitchen and about knocked me down while trying to get to Jackie. They loved her so much and so did I. She was my best friend in the world.

Kelly stretched her neck, looking around at me. "Where's our snack, Grandma?"

"It's coming right up" I replied.

The girls and Jackie played until it was time for dinner and Jackie ate with us, and then went home for the night. We were going to try again tomorrow and, hopefully, this time we would get what we needed. Time was running out. The court date was next month. We had to come up with something soon. Bedtime came quickly and I was ready for it. I was exhausted and ready for a goodnight sleep.

***

Crying out, I sprang to a sitting position in bed, clutching the covers at my neck. The same dream again. Why was I dreaming this every night? A tear slid down my cheek and I wiped it. How long had I been crying? Apparently, the dream caused more heartache than I'd been prepared for. Lying back, I clutched my pillow to my chest and rocked. Sleep finally came once more.

When I awoke again, I dragged myself out of bed and let Kelly help me get Amy dressed for the day. Glancing in the mirror, the pink and white dress added to her complexion and brightened her face. Unfortunately, it didn't do anything to lift my spirits or erase the throbbing headache from my horrible dream.

"Did you have that bad dream again?" Jackie asked when she came in. I looked at her and the look in her eyes made me look away. I hated when Jackie looked at me with worry in her eyes.

"Susan, you can tell me about it," Jackie

said.

"I know I can," I said. "It's no big deal. It's just a dream."

"Are you stressed out right now? Because of Tina? I wish you would talk to me more."

I loved Jackie like a big sister and a protective friend who had my back. I wished I could talk about the dreams. I just couldn't talk about them until I understood them better.

"Promise me you're okay," she said. "That you're not... you know... losing it..."

"Jackie, I swear I am not losing it. Okay, listen, we have to get ready," I said. "We're leaving in an hour, sharp. I want to get this over with."

We got the girls off to school and had our morning coffee. It was time to get the proof we needed. Today was going to be our day of success; I just knew it.

***

"Jackie after we get this today, we need to go out and have some fun together. Something that will get our minds off all this. I need to go out and have fun. Have a few drinks, without having to worry about anything. Talk to guys, flirt with guys, and push my limits even." Plus, if I was drunk

31

enough then maybe I could get a full night's sleep without having that damn nightmare again. "I want to go out. Who's driving?"

"I will drive; I don't need to be drunk to have fun," Jackie said.

I smiled. "You have a deal, Jackie."

I felt guilty thinking about it, but it made me somewhat happy to have a night out with Jackie. "Come on. We need to get this started."

Jackie and I left to go find Tina one more time. I was hoping this time I could get a picture of her getting the drugs. On the drive over, Jackie and I didn't say much. Twenty minutes later, we found ourselves outside her house once more. A flicker of movement in the window told me she was home. More time passed, my cup of coffee grew even colder. I was wondering how long we would have to sit and watch when she came out the front door. She was noticeably thin, drops of water clinging to her face, but she held her head high as she walked.

Of course, she had gone back to the same alley again. I would have to be very careful this time. I told Jackie to stay in the car until I returned. "Are you sure you can do this, Susan?" Jackie said

"Yes, I can do this. I promised."

I started into the alley. It seemed darker this time. The ball of nerves that always appeared when I was around darkness began to form in my stomach and I had to force myself to continue. I fanned my face with a piece of paper. *Get a grip*, I told myself. I walked further into the darkness. The deep rumble of voices sent shivers through me and I struggled to hide. I wanted to blink, to look away, but felt unable to move. I had to do this; I needed the proof. There was no expression on her face; she was stone-faced, completely unmoved. Loudly, she cursed him. Wanting the encounter over, I stepped out far enough to get a picture of him handing her the drugs. I had forgotten all about the flash on the camera. They both turned and looked at me when the flash went off.

I turned and ran as fast as I could. His grip was firm; the feel of his palm against my bare flesh was enough to make me scream out loud. I fought him off and started running for the car. Jackie must have seen me coming, because she had the car running as I opened the door.

"Did you get it?" Jackie said.

"Go, Jackie!" I yelled.

She floored the gas and spun out. "Well? Did you get the picture?" she asked again.

"I got it," I replied with a grin.

Chapter Four

Who is this man?

When I woke up the next morning, it was as though I never went to sleep. I was tired, uncomfortable, and I tried to recall the dreams I had last night but my mind wouldn't let me. Bits and pieces came to me throughout the entire morning as I got the girls ready for school. Today was an easy day: laundry, cleaning, and cooking, in that order. Then later that night, Jackie and I were going to have a girl's night out. Jackie came over earlier than I thought she would.

"Are you okay?" I asked her.

"No," she said. "I have a headache. I think I am getting sick."

"How much did you eat last night?"

"Not much. I think it is a stomach bug or something," she replied in a solemn voice.

"A stomach bug. How did you get a stomach bug?" I asked.

Jackie half smiled and rushed into the

kitchen when her nose caught the scent of coffee. I had to laugh because that was what Jackie always did when she didn't want to go somewhere. She would pretend to be sick. It was bad food, bad sleep, or some kind of made up illness like a stomach bug. I wasn't going to call her out on it. I found her sitting at my small kitchen table, sipping coffee, dazing off.

"How was last night; did you get any sleep?" I asked.

Jackie looked at me and smiled. "You know, the usual lack of sleep."

I went for the coffee, too, and thought about Jackie's night. She never had any fun. If she got a little wild, enjoyed herself, she would sleep very well. That was what I wanted. That was why I wanted to go out tonight. It wasn't to get caught in a romance or to sleep with anyone. I poured my coffee and knew it was time. Confession time, I turned with my cup and walked to the table. I poured creamer into the coffee, watching the black and white mix together. That was the way I loved my coffee. Too much creamer and the coffee would have no kick. Too little creamer and it would be too bitter. Add a little sugar and the magical potion was perfect and ready for consumption.

I opened my mouth and something

opposite to what I wanted to say came out. "Jackie, you need a life." Jackie paused in mid sip, her eyes wide. After a few seconds, she took her drink and then put the mug on the table. She licked her lips and exhaled.

"Whoa," she said.

"Whoa? That's it? Whoa?"

"Give me a second to absorb that," Jackie said. "So I don't have a life?"

"You have a life; you just need more of one," I said.

"I know that. That's what scares me because I have not been out for a very long time and I have not been with a man in a long time. I couldn't say that with a straight face." Jackie smiled.

"Do you like going out?"

"Of course I do. I love having fun."

"Who said it has to be a relationship? Why can't you just have fun with a guy?" I asked.

"There's no way it can be something sexual and casual," she said.

Jackie smiled. Smiled so big, I swore I could see the corners of her mouth curling up. She loved

36

this. "Still thinking about going tonight, huh?" I grinned

"I don't know," Jackie said. "I'm just confused."

I stood up. I made up my mind to dump my coffee—which was no easy feat, because I wanted to cry from getting rid of the magic—finish getting my chores done, and call the baby sitter. But I couldn't. I kept talking, even as I stood there, trying to talk Jackie into going with me tonight. I finally talked her into going. I finished getting all my chores done and waited for Jackie. I didn't feel like going alone tonight so I was glad she decided to go with me. The babysitter had already arrived, so I was just waiting on Jackie to get there. As I was waiting, I copied the picture that I got of Tina onto the computer. I didn't know who the man was in the photo, but I really wasn't worried about him. I just needed the proof she was still using.

Jackie drove and before we could even back up, she asked, "What are we going to do?"

"You're going to have the best time of your life!"

Judging by the way Jackie raised an eyebrow, I hadn't convinced her. Hell, I hadn't convinced myself.

We crept into the bar just as one of the bands took the stage. I heard the sound of drumsticks tapping together and then the first notes of a love song began. There was a guy at the bar and I couldn't help staring at him. He caught me and smiled. He turned and motioned for the bartender. She was a tall red head with a chest like mine. She bent over, way too far, letting her chest basically pour from her slutty tank top. I couldn't believe it, but I was actually jealous right then. I felt the sting in my nerves, thinking this handsome stranger was flirting with her, or making plans to go home with her.

As I stood, I knew my body was in the mood for something with this guy. I would take it slow and see how it went. Jackie and I found a table to sit at. We ordered our drinks, a sex on the beach for me and Jackie had a coke. I noticed he kept staring at me. I would glance up every now and then to see if he was still looking at me. The next time I looked up, he was walking toward us. I could feel the butterflies in my stomach start to flutter. All I could manage was a curt nod and a meager attempt at a smile that felt more like a nervous twitch. He asked if he could join us. I nodded.

"Would you care for something else to drink?" he asked.

"No thank..." I stopped midsentence. Why

not?

I wasn't going to be watching everyone else enjoy themselves? Jackie was right. I deserved some fun. "Here you go." The bartender set the tall glass of long island ice tea on the table. I had always wanted to try this. "What is your name?" I asked him.

"Dave. What is your name?" Dave whispered.

"Susan," I said, "and this is Jackie."

That voice. Deep and low and sexy, the sound turned every ounce of me to mush.

"Do I know you from somewhere?"

"I don't think so; I would remember if we had met before," I teased him.

His cell phone rang, and he picked it up and started talking to someone. The music was too loud so I couldn't hear what he was saying. He looked at me in a strange way as he was talking. He hung his phone up and looked at me and said, "Who are you kidding? I know who you are. You are the one who took the picture of me and Tina in the alley." I froze, but said nothing and waited for him to continue. "I want that picture," he said in a threatening way.

"Susan!" Jackie yelled. "We need to get out of here now."

"Are you okay, ladies?" the security guard's voice wrenched out of nowhere.

Dave got up and left the bar quickly when the security guard came toward us. Damn it. We told the guard we were fine and everything was okay. Jackie wanted to hurry and leave before Dave could return, so we got up and headed for the car. The first blow had knocked my head into the ground, stunning me. The kick to my side had me gasping for air. I could hear Jackie fighting him. I rolled over to see what was happening. He was hitting her ribs as he continued kicking her. As her consciousness had begun to fade, the beating had become almost unbearable to watch. I couldn't move and I couldn't help her. I could barely move and my breath came in shallow gasps as the damage to my ribs threatened to rob what little air I had left.

I tried to reach her, the sound of short gasping breaths as she struggled for air the only thing to be heard. I listened for his footsteps to make sure he wasn't coming back. I pulled myself closer to Jackie to see if she was alright.

Her shallow breath slowed as she struggled and whispered, "Why?"

I reached for her and felt her go limp. "Jackie!" I screamed as loud as I could. "No!" The anger that welled up inside of me gave me strength to crawl to the entrance of the bar to get help. A guy coming out of the bar frantically pulled out his cell phone and called 9-1-1. He tried to calm me, but I just pulled desperately at his shirt. After quickly identifying himself to the dispatcher, he quickly gave our location and turned back to me. "Jackie... God...Help her," I forced the words out through gritted teeth.

"Oh shit! Please, don't try to move, okay? Help is on the way." He gently brushed the tears away from her eyes. Taking his jacket off, he covered her to keep her warm.

***

Officer John Davis had never seen someone slashed as brutally as Jackie had been. The ambulance finally arrived and took Jackie to the hospital. I followed in the other ambulance.

"No!" Grabbing at my sweat soaked sheets, I panted in the morning light; staring at the ceiling, thankful for whatever had woken me up. My heart was racing from that damned nightmare. Disoriented, I tried to place where I was at. I was at the hospital and last night really happened.

My nurse walked in as I was remembering

41

what happened. "Are you okay, Mrs. Green?" she asked.

"I'm fine, How is my friend Jackie?" I replied.

"We have her stable, but unfortunately she is in a coma," she replied.

"What about the girls!?" I yelled.

I had to call the babysitter to let her know what happened. I grabbed the phone and called the house. Kathy answered the phone right away. I explained everything to her and asked her if she could look after them until I could come home. I had known Kathy since she was a little girl and I trusted her with the girls. She told me she would stay with them until I returned and she was very sorry about Jackie. Hearing her name made me turn to see if the nurse was still in my room.

She smiled warmly at me and said, "Would you like to see her?"

"Yes," I replied.

After she'd wheeled me to a room down the hall, I looked at Jackie laying there and I couldn't hold back my shock. I started to sob. My heart felt like it was going to break in half. The doctor walked in and introduced himself. "I am

Harold Jones and I will be her doctor," he said. "They haven't finished the entire test so right now we're just making some educated guesses." He told me that the coma was most likely produced by the head injury. He also said she could wake up anytime or it could be days until she regained conscious. He did say there was swelling in her brain. He left the room and I sat back, deep in thought. I had a bad feeling about the whole thing and didn't for one minute think that this was the end of it. That guy, Dave was obviously determined to get that picture back.

A familiar voice interrupted my train of thought. Turning in my seat, I watched Fay enter the room, beautiful as ever as she made her way toward me. How did she know I was here? "Asshole," she muttered. She turned to me and told me that the hospital had called her because she was my emergency contact. "They said you were mugged, Mom," she said in anger. I didn't want her to know what Jackie and I were doing so I just agreed that we were mugged. The pain had been so intense that even the *Demerol* they were giving me wasn't touching it, so Fay asked them to give me something stronger. They made me go back to my room, but I didn't want to leave Jackie. The nurse promised me if she woke up she would come and get me. Fay stayed with me until I fell asleep from the medication they gave me.

***

The nurse startled me when she entered my room. "Sorry, I guess I'm just a little on edge. Plus, I'm worried about my friend," I said.

"No apologies necessary; you have every right to be on edge, and your friend is still the same," she told me. She asked how my pain level was. I told her it wasn't that bad right now. "How are you, really?" she replied.

"I am fine, really," I said.

Kathy had called and said she would bring the girls over to see me. She said they were worried. I told her that would be fine because I knew if Kelly didn't get to see me, she would worry herself sick. My oldest granddaughter always tried to be serious; her thinking was that now that she was the ripe old age of eight she had to be grown up.

It was earlier than she had planned to drop the girls off, but she had some errands to run and figured the girls would rather be with me while she accomplished them. She would return for them after she got everything done. "I just texted your Fay, and she said she is on her way over now," Kathy said before she left.

Smiling at the girls, I motioned for them to

44

come to me. I placed a kiss on both of their foreheads. Kelly asked me where Jackie was. I told her she was sick and would be away for a little while. She was not old enough to understand what had happened.

Drumming her fingers on the bed table, Kelly looked at the banana I had earlier that morning. "Yes, Kelly, you may have it," I said, knowing exactly what she was thinking but not vocalizing.

"Hey Kelly!" Fay yelled as she entered the room. She startled Kelly and she dropped the banana on the floor. Laughing, she helped her gather up the smashed banana off the floor. She pulled something out of a brown paper bag. "Coffee?" she said.

"Now you know that's the magic word. "I replied. I sipped my coffee and stared at Fay. She had grown so much in the past four months. I thought they stopped growing when they hit eighteen. "Hmm... I'm sorry, what did you say?"

"I asked when you were getting out of here?" she replied back.

I really didn't know yet. "The doctor has not been in to see me yet."

She couldn't stay long she had to get back

to school. "I hope you can come see me at home next weekend," I said, practically begging.

"Sure, maybe next weekend. We'll see how the week goes, okay?"

"Okay, call me this week and let me know," I replied. "And perhaps convince your brother to come along as well," I hinted.

***

The rest of the day passed quickly, with the exception of the reaming I received from my doctor. He was insistent that I rest and that the children be taken home. Kathy had come and picked them up an hour ago. I wanted to go see Jackie so I rang for my nurse. She came into my room and walked me down to where Jackie was. I sat in the chair beside her and began to beg her to wake up. It didn't take long for me to realize that she wasn't going to respond. This was entirely my fault. *Why did I ever get you involved in this? I can't lose you Jackie you are my strength and my best friend.* With tears in my eyes, I realized I could lose her forever. Grade two concussion and four staples in my head and cracked ribs was nothing compared to what Jackie was going through. Why couldn't this be me instead of her?

I was heartbroken at the effect this was having on the girls also. Tears rolled down my face as I thought about how they must have felt when they saw me today and when I told them that Jackie would be away for a while. Closing my eyes, I let the pounding in my head beat a steady rhythm as I tried to get my emotions in check. My grandkids were my whole life and I knew how badly their mother's actions had impacted them and now I was running around putting Jackie's life in danger and my own as well. I had to go back to my room and try to get myself together. I kissed Jackie on the forehead and left for my room. I asked the nurse to let me know if Jackie happened to wake up. I was feeling drained. I didn't know if I would make it back to my room or not.

I fell on my bed and that was the last thing I remembered until I woke up to the nurse bringing me my breakfast. I was hoping the doctor would release me today so I could get home to the girls. I didn't want to leave Jackie, but the girls needed me. I could always come over here after the girls went to school.

My doctor came in right after breakfast and told me I could go home. I thanked him profusely and then I called Kathy to see if she could come and get me. I was used to Jackie always being the person who came and got me. It brought tears to my eyes knowing she might never get to do that again. I made sure that my nurse wrote down my number just in case Jackie woke up. That way they could contact me so I could get over here. My head was pounding again and the four staples on the back of my head itched, but I didn't care because I was going home. I just had to wait to get my release from the nurse.

I stopped in to see Jackie before I left. She was white as a ghost. I leaned down and whispered in her ear. "Come back to me, Jackie. I need you. I love you. Come back, please."

Chapter Five

Jackie's battle

"Mamaw!" Kelly barreled into me, grabbing me tightly around the waist. Leaning into my granddaughter, I could feel the tears threatening to fall. Amy followed a bit more sedately, but hugged me just as hard. Kissing the top of their heads, I realized just how much this incident had affected them.

"Kelly, Amy, have you guys behaved for Kathy?" I looked past them at Kathy, who was standing in the doorway with her arms crossed. I knew what that meant as soon as I saw her. Kelly smiled as she looked at her; Kelly was a carbon copy of her mother, right down to trying to be tough. But she wasn't. She asked me if I was alright. "I am okay, just a couple of staples that's all." The look my granddaughter gave me said it all. Kelly knew that wasn't all and she knew there was more going on, but she knew better than to ask.

***

The next morning after the girls had left I went straight to the hospital. As I arrived at Jackie's room, I saw it was empty. I ran to the information

49

desk and waited as the attendant talked on her cell phone. She raised a finger, signaling for me to wait, and laughing, she said, "I can't believe he said that to you!"

My impatience hit a high note and I snatched the phone from her. "Jackie O'Conner. She was brought in the other day. Where is she?"

"Ma'am," she began, "do not touch me again or I will call security."

I slammed the cell on the counter. "Do that, and I'll call your supervisor to make sure they know your personal calls take priority over patient business. Find out where she is or I'll have your ass fired before the end of your shift."

Her nostrils flared angrily, but looked on the computer. She buzzed me in and reached calmly for her cell phone as I walked through the opening double doors. I rarely resorted to being a bitch in order to get what I wanted, but my whole life was behind that door and I didn't give a shit what anybody thought of me then.

"Excuse me," I said, slowing to ask a passing nurse, "I'm looking for Jackie O'Conner; she was transferred to this floor a while ago."

"I'm sorry, I don't know," she said politely. "You'll have to ask the nurse's station. It's just around the corner to your left."

I ran down the hall to the nurse's station. "Excuse me," I said loudly, "Jackie O'Conner, what room is she in?" The nurse looked up from her binder and nodded at the room behind her. "Why was she moved?"

"We're not exactly sure yet," the nurse offered sympathetically. "She had problems breathing last night. They think a fracture blocked her airway; they've got her on a ventilator. I'm sorry, but that's about all I know at this point. I promise as soon as I know something, I'll be in to speak with you."

I walked in the room and saw Jackie on the ventilator and I fell to my knees. Seeing Jackie in that room, strapped to the bed with hoses running all over her and machines beeping, was agony. It reminded me of Tina.

"Wake up, Jackie, please. Jackie, please talk to me," I begged.

My stomach knotted while I waited for her to say something, anything. I couldn't lose her. There had to be something I could do to get her to wake up. I stood by her bed and started talking to her. I told her about how the girls missed her and she had to wake up so they could see her. I stood there for hours talking to her, but she didn't respond. The nurse told me to keep talking to her, that she could hear me. I stayed the whole day with her, but I had to get home for the girls.

My head pounded after leaving, so I stopped at the pharmacy on my way back home to grab a bottle of water and something for the headache. I was walking down the pain relief aisle when my phone buzzed and I slowed to read the texts, but then the front door chimed again, and I glanced up with my jaw shut tight and the hair on my arms standing up, like a shot of electricity was shooting through me at the sight of him. It was that Dave guy from the alley. It had to be now, when I was at my most vulnerable? What kind of a cruel joke was the universe playing on me? I hadn't imagined I'd run into him again.

I wanted to reach over and yank him by the hair, pull his face to mine, curse him for all the pain he'd caused. I wanted him to know what true suffering really felt like. I couldn't find the strength to do it. I ran out the side door. I ran the entire way to the car in my heels, jumping over the cracked, uneven concrete on the sidewalk. I about twisted my ankles a few times. It took me ten minutes to catch my breath as I drove home. The fears that overcame me were so strong they over powered the hate that I felt for the man. I was still shaking. I needed to pull it together before the girls got home. I felt so alone without Jackie. She was my rock to lean on when things went wrong and I didn't have her now. I could hear Jackie's voice in my head saying, "Suck it up, Susan! You can do this on your own." Could I? Was I strong enough?

***

The next day, Tuesday, I slowly pulled my blue jeans up and put on my freshly ironed white shirt. Luckily, I had both long and short sleeved shirts, and though I would look a little ridiculous wearing a long sleeved shirt on a warm September day, it was more important that I hide the handprint bruises that were on both my arms. The good news was, they were no longer causing me any pain. I bruised easily, but healed quickly. Long sleeves in warm weather were a crazy idea, but I didn't want the girls to see the bruises and start asking questions. I gently rolled Kelly and Amy out of bed, sitting them up and gently telling them it was time to get ready for school as they rubbed sleep from their eyes. When they were finished, they groggily tumbled into the clothes I had laid out for them on their stand.

I had already filled two bowls with corn flakes in the kitchen when I started my coffee brewing. After they ate, they left for school. It was a familiar routine, one I had been doing for as long back as I could remember; even with my own children. After they had left, I took a deep breath and forced myself to move. I needed to call the bakery and let them know I wouldn't be in for a while and then I needed to get to the hospital. It was my turn to be there for Jackie. I don't get close to anyone, I don't associate with them unless I had to, and I mean *absolutely* had to. At my age, I had seen and came into contact with countless people, but never, never ever had I gotten to know someone, and become friends with anyone, the way I had with Jackie.

The thought of losing her scared me to death. My heart leapt in my chest so violently I thought I was having a mini heart attack. I had to get myself under control so I could get to the hospital to be with her. How did this happen? The question kept wandering through my mind. A tear trailed down my cheek and I quickly wiped it away. I had to stay strong. But I felt completely lost. It felt like I was drowning and I couldn't catch my breath. That pretty much described my days lately. I headed out the door and got into my car. My car revved to life. Placing my hands on the steering wheel, I told myself, *you can do this, Susan.*

I pulled into the hospital's parking lot and turned my car off. I sat there for a few minutes to get myself together. As I entered the hospital, I began to feel shaky all over. I stopped for a minute to calm myself. *Come on, Susan, you can do this*. I went to Jackie's room and I was in shock as to what I saw. Jackie's eyes were opened. I ran to get the nurse. She told me she had woken up about ten minutes ago and she tried to call me but there was no answer. My heart skipped a beat at this news. It was not something I was expecting. I slowly asked, "Has she spoken?" She reminded me that she couldn't because of the ventilator. I should have known that. I was so happy to see her eyes open. I sat beside her and talked her head off. She would nod every now and then to let me know she understood what I was saying. She started pointing at her feet for some reason. I didn't know what she wanted so I got her nurse. The nurse came in and checked her feet. Every time she touched them, Jackie shook her head no. *Oh my god*. She couldn't feel her legs.

The clouds were depressing, a true grey day, and perfect to go with my sudden, depressive mood. It was going to be the day things turned around, I was so sure. Everything just turned in the opposite direction I was hoping for. I would be happy if I could just push the delete button for the past few days and forget any of this ever happened. Jackie never shed a tear; she was such a strong person. She glanced quickly at me, frowning, and then looked forward while shaking her head, like she was telling me not to cry. I wiped the tears from my eyes and quickly calmed myself. I asked the doctor when he came in if this was going to be permanent. He told me he couldn't tell until the swelling went down. He went over to talk to Jackie and explain to her what was going on. All she could do was nod her head.

I told her I was going to get coffee and I would be right back. As I turned to leave, I had the distinct feeling that someone was watching me. It occurred to me that I had felt it all throughout the day, but had been too consumed to notice or really care. A sound behind me startled me. I turned to the direction of the sound and saw a figure advance from behind the double doors. In the shadows, I could tell that it was a woman's figure. I had to look quick because as she saw me look, she turned and ran. "Tina," I yelled. I really couldn't tell if it was her, but it looked like her. Why would she be here?

She was the last person I ever expected to see at all, until the court date at least. Maybe it wasn't her; maybe I startled the person and she ran away. I just ignored it and went to get my coffee so I could get back to Jackie. She needed me now and I was going to be there for her, no matter what. I had pulled my hair up into a clip when I was in the cafeteria, trying to figure out how to use all the buttons on the coffee pot/espresso maker, and I was able to get a full cup of coffee this time without spilling it. I could never work this thing without spilling half of my coffee. I was proud of myself. Jackie always laughed at me when I did it.

I realized I hadn't eaten a single thing all day, but it was too late to do anything about it now. I had to hurry and get back so I could spend some time with Jackie before I had to leave for home. Whether I was willing to face it or not, I knew that there was a chance Jackie would never walk again. Grabbing my head and massaging my temples with my thumbs, I squeezed my eyes shut and wished for all this to go away. To avoid odd stares from others, I tried my best to keep my emotions in check.

"Miss Green, are you alright?" the booming voice of a young nurse interrupted my thoughts, bringing me back to the present. I looked up and nodded quietly, unable to keep the sorrow from my face. Instinctively, I wrapped my arms around my waist in a desperate attempt to hold myself together. I told the young lady I was fine and walked back to Jackie's room.

***

"Oh my, look at that hair," I told Jackie. I fixed her hair and I talked her ear off the whole time. After a while I knew I was getting on her nerves so I decided to go home. I just didn't know what to say to her. I felt so guilty and all I wanted to keep saying was I'm sorry. I kissed her forehead and told her I would be back tomorrow to check on her. She nodded her head and I left. Standing outside the room door, I closed my eyes as the images of that day's events flashed through my mind. I shook my head in an attempt to clear them away.

The afternoon sun beamed down on me as I went out the double doors of the exit, making me squint at the brightness. It was the middle of November, and almost time for school to close for the holidays. I started the engine and my rusty old car roared to life. Holding Jackie's hand while she lay broken and battered in the hospital bed today, I couldn't begin to fathom what my life was going to be like if she didn't make it. As strong as Jackie was, I knew it took all of her strength to even try to hold on. I wanted to take that pain away and keep it as my own. No one should ever have to go through this. I sat there for the longest time before heading home.

I started to back out of the parking lot. When I sidled down the road, I took one last look in the rearview mirror. I really didn't want to leave her, but I had to. If I knew that my life was going to take an abrupt roller coaster ride and shift into something much different than what it was at this very moment, I would've stayed home that day and never worried about getting the proof I needed. My sleep was fitful at best, plagued with a persistent nightmare that had me terrified of closing my eyes because as soon as I did, I slipped back into the nightmare world. I wish I could get a good night's rest.

I pulled into the driveway and got out of the car. The house looked so inviting after a long day at the hospital. The girls were getting off the bus as I approached the porch. As they saw me, they came running to me and kissed me and hugged me tight. Their hugs always made everything bad go away. I was smiling again after all the sadness of the day. We went in and I started dinner right away. The girls went upstairs to play until it was done. Amy came running into the kitchen and asked what I had cooked.

"Miss Amy, I cooked everything you like. Can I serve you a plate?" I asked, pulling out a chair for her to sit.

After getting the girls settled, I fixed myself a plate, and I started eating so fast I nearly forgot the girls were eating with me. When I looked up, Kelly was watching me. Where did I get this appetite from? If I kept eating like that, I'd need a new diet plan in about a week.

"Slow down. We're not going to steal anything from you," Kelly said, laughing.

Everybody else at the table joined in the laughter. It felt great to be able to laugh again even if it was for just a moment.

***

One Month Later…

I felt as if I was stuck in time. My life was on hold until the trial was over. I was due to give evidence via video link, because I couldn't stand the thought of being in the same room as her, but the more I thought about it the more I thought. about what Jackie said before the accident. Jackie had gone in depth a million times about finding closure. She asked me to think about what it would take for me to be able to put it behind me enough to move forward. Following her instructions, I had been thinking about it over the past month, but there was nothing. Not until the trial date was set and my lawyer spoke about how I could give evidence of her buying drugs. Jackie seemed to think facing her could offer the closure I needed, but she also asked me to consider what I would do or how I would feel if Tina won. Devastated. Scared. To think that a judge could possibly believe that she was clean and ready to take care of the children would be devastating.

I didn't know how I would handle it. There was also something else to consider, or someone else–the girls. Jackie talked about the judge seeing through Tina's charm. No one did for years. Not even the people closest to her. How were strangers going to? I couldn't think like that. There was evidence on my laptop that proved she had bought drugs that day. I wished it was already over. My throat burned, and I swallowed hard to try to stop myself from crying, but it was no use. I kept thinking about what Jackie had said. I tried not to let any doubt enter my mind, but when she said things like that, I couldn't help it.

I groaned and ran my hands over my face. Going over it again wasn't helping. I had made the decision and I had to live with it, and so did Tina. Soon enough, though, I'd get to see whether Jackie felt I'd done the right thing, or if I'd made the biggest mistake of both of our lives. Grabbing my mail from the side table, I escaped to my room. Having the girls around was great, but at the end of the day I was exhausted. They had too much energy. I flopped down on the bed and ripped the first envelope open. *Please have something decent in here.* There were just bills, as always. The trial was starting soon.

At first, I didn't want to go. I didn't want to hear the details. I had given a full statement of what happened the day we followed her and it was going to be read out in court. Now, though, I wanted to be there. I needed to watch her go down, and I wanted to see her again. Collapsing on my bed, I squeezed my eyes shut. I needed sleep badly.

Tomorrow was another day of visiting Jackie and praying she would get better. I laid across the bed and within seconds I was asleep. The dreams came once more in the night and scared me to death. After waking from the first one, I went back to sleep and slept the whole night. I couldn't remember this dream, though. Maybe that was a good thing.

Chapter six

Jackie comes home

After our morning of laughing and carrying on with the girls, I made my way to the hospital to see how Jackie was doing. On the drive over I hoped and prayed they would have some good news to tell me. I went straight up to her room, when I heard the most wonderful sound I could ever hear. My stomach flipped over. I had missed the sound of her voice so much. Let's face it, I had missed everything about her. She was yelling at the nurse to bring her some coffee. I stood still and stared at her, and she did the same. There was so much I wanted to say that I couldn't figure out what to open with.

So she started with, "Look what I can do." She wiggled her big toe and laughed. "I'm fine," she said, laughing and shaking her head at me. I had missed the sound of her laugh, too. I could hear it in my head, but the real thing was so much better.

"Oh my God! I'm so glad you're doing better." Jackie told me that the doctor said it was the swelling that stopped her from feeling her legs. The swelling was going down and she could feel them again. She laughed quietly, making my heart race. That was the first time I'd heard her laugh properly in years. I couldn't help smiling like an idiot. She glanced at me out of the corner of her eye. I smiled, and she smiled back. It was almost too intense. The atmosphere around us felt like... I didn't even know how to explain it. Everything just felt right again.

She looked at me as if I'd grown a second head. "You're kidding, right? Have you seen how hot the doctors are in this hospital?" Grinning, I went back to sit down. Jackie pushed her call button and asked to see her doctor.

"Why do you want to see him?" I asked.

"Just wait and see, Susan, you will know why."

When he entered the room his eyes flickered to my lips, and my heart skipped a beat. Everything else disappeared, and all I could see was his beautiful face. Was this a good idea, though? We'd only just met. I closed my eyes and took a deep breath. That wasn't easy to do. He walked over to Jackie and asked her if there was something wrong. Jackie just said, "No, I wanted you to meet my best friend, Susan. Susan, this is Robert Deems"

He walked over to me. Suddenly I realized how close he was. Our faces were inches apart. My breath caught in my throat as he stared into my eyes.

"Hello. Jackie has told me a lot about you." Robert said. "She told me you are a nurse and you also raise your two granddaughters."

I couldn't believe Jackie had told him all of that. I knew what she was up to. He asked me if I would like to get a cup of coffee and talk while he was on lunch break. Of course I told him yes. We sat and talked way passed his lunch break. His pager went off and he glanced down at it and told me he had to go back to work, but he really wanted to spend more time with me.

"Do you have any plans this weekend? You want to come with me this weekend to look for a boat?" Robert asked, changing the subject before he started laughing. "I could use another opinion. Apparently, I'm too negative when it comes to buying a boat."

"Yeah? I'd love to," I replied. This was happening so fast but felt so right. I knew it wasn't a date or anything, but I was still excited to spend time with him. Jackie had a smile on her face when I told her about it.

His arm brushed against mine as he walked

out of the room. My breath caught in my throat. This was so nice, so normal again. I didn't want our talk to come to an end. I loved boats and to be able to ride on one was going to be amazing. That is if he asked me to go sailing. I went back to Jackie's room. I looked at Jackie and instead of voicing my opinion, I smiled and received one in return. My heart raced. Yes, I definitely wanted him. Jackie and I sat and talked all day until it was time for me to leave. Robert came back in and gave me his number and got my number. He also said Jackie might be able to come home in a few days. It had been a wonderful day. She smiled, and her eyes lit up. My fingers brushed over his as he took the phone. There was a small smile on his lips and a blush on his cheeks as we touched. It was good to know that he felt the same. I watched him closely as he punched his number in my phone. I couldn't believe I actually survived this. "Done," he announced, handing me the phone back. I made sure my fingers touched his again and like last time, his cheeks flushed. "Feel special now?"

I pretended to think about it for a minute. "No. You're going to have to do a lot more than that to make me feel special." He raised his eyebrow and tried to stop himself from smiling.

"Really?" He nodded, my eyes lingering over his lips. "Alright," he said, giving me a cute smile that made my heart stop.

I told Jackie I had to get home to do some cleaning before the girls got in. I also had to call the bakery to check in. We hugged and said our good byes and I left. I drove back to my house with the biggest smile on my face. This day couldn't get better. Well, it could if he turned up naked in my room. *Stop it*, I admonished myself. I pulled into my driveway; I didn't need to think about stuff like that right now. I heard the phone ringing so I ran to the house and picked it up.

It was Robert and all he said was, "I'll pick you up at eight on Saturday. Wear something short," he said, hanging up and laughing to himself. I bet he was blushing.

***

I cleaned house later that day, feeling happier than I had in a long time. I felt like a helium balloon was growing inside of me and I might just float away. I was so happy. Things were going to get better. The girls even said I was very happy today. I told them that Jackie might be coming home soon. They were so excited at the news.

***

I lay in bed that night feeling a giddy excitement flowing through me. It wasn't just the excitement of going on a so called date, but that I was going to do this with David. It was the perfect excuse to spend time with him. Helping him buy a boat and then maybe go out on the boat. I fell asleep thinking of him and I slept like a baby.

***

The next few days had gone by in a blur. First the surprise date night for Robert and I. That had gone surprisingly well. Awkward, but it had worked. Before I knew it we were on a second date and this time we went on the boat. I had looked so cute in my little blue jacket; cute and obviously cold. I hadn't meant to, but my arms had wrapped around his so easily to keep me warm. I had nestled into him, fitting in his arms like he had always been there. Fireworks had lit up the sky, but I didn't see them. All I saw was Robert. He had turned his head to look at me, the scent of his cologne filling my world. How many times had I denied myself something I wanted? And here was the person I wanted most, his lips an inch away and holding onto me like he needed me. I had leaned forward and kissed him. It had been perfect.

And then the lights came back on and I came crashing back into reality. I wished the firework show could have lasted forever, because then I could have kissed him forever. Instead, the harsh light of the lake exposed the broken moment

68

as something that I could never have. The night was over and I didn't want it to be. Robert parked the boat in the docks and we went to his car. The whole way home I thought of that kiss. I wanted to take things slow, but the feelings that were growing were amazing. He walked me to my door and I waited to see if he would kiss me again and he did. His lips were so soft and gentle. I didn't want to let go. He said goodnight and said he would call me.

***

My alarm began beeping and I groaned and rolled out of bed. I didn't want to leave the warm blankets that I could pretend had David in them if I closed my eyes. I slid on a pair of mostly clean jeans and a long sleeved shirt and headed downstairs. I ran my fingers through my hair, reminding myself that I really needed to get a haircut. I got the girls ready for school and headed to the hospital to get Jackie. She was coming home. David was releasing her at noon. She would be in a wheel chair for a little while until she went through physical therapy.

I hadn't eaten anything yet, so I drove over to the coffee shop by the hospital and ordered a breakfast sandwich. I looked out at the hospital and wondered if Robert was working. What was I going to say to him today? I had no idea what to say to him. *Hey Robert, I really enjoyed kissing you last night. I've wanted to kiss you since the day I met you. Would you mind terribly just making out with me?* Yeah, that would sound very mature. I finished my sandwich and decided to go ahead and head over to the hospital. It was early, but it would give me a chance to talk to Jackie.

The car was still warm as I slid into the seat and headed back to the hospital. I pulled into the parking lot and headed inside, my thoughts on how to rearrange my schedule so I could take care of Jackie until she was better.

As I walked into Jackie's room, I heard his voice and I started to walk faster. I couldn't wait to see him again. Our eyes connected, and I felt a surge of electricity power through my body. I wondered if he felt the same way I did about our kiss. I prayed silently that he did. He got done talking to Jackie and turned to me and said, "I will call you as soon as I can get time away from this hospital."

I just looked at him and replied, "That's fine." He smiled and walked out of the room. My world shattered. He didn't want me. The promise was an easy way to turn me down without hurting me. But it did hurt, more than he could possibly know.

I closed my eyes and permitted myself a rare moment to breathe deeply; I had to pull myself together. I really had to stop falling so hard so quickly. "Morning, Jackie." I tossed my bag on the chair and walked over to the bed, where I hopped up on the side, propping my elbow on Jackie. "You ready to break out of this joint?" I asked her.

She was more than ready. "Why don't you ask him out for dinner?" Jackie said.

"No," I replied. "I will not make a fool of myself. If he wants to go out again, he will call me."

"Ok I won't mention it again," she said.

I had become accustomed to being used and had given up on finding real love. I had reached a point in my life that I wasn't even sure there was such a thing as unconditional love except for that of a love between a parent and their child. I had tried it all; bars, blind dates, and even online dating sites.

The only thing I ever found in a bar was a one night stand, which I didn't believe in. Friends fixed me up with their friends, but it never went further than one date. Online dating sites were full of desperate people and desperation was not a foundation for a long term relationship.

Quite frankly, I had gotten tired of feeling used, so I convinced myself there was no such thing as love... Why did I have to meet him?

"What's the matter, Susan? Why the tears? This is a happy time. We're out of here and on our way home in just a few hours," Jackie said.

We waited on the nurse to release her and I packed her belongings that she was taking home with her. Jackie was going to stay at her home; she would never stay with me because it would make her feel like she was a burden. I was going to stay with her during the day to make sure she had everything she needed.

Time flew by. Honestly, I could not remember. Most of the day passed so fast it wasn't much more than a blur. There were only a few things I vividly remember. One was how I felt when Robert blew me off. I got Jackie settled in for the night and the girls and I went home.

A leisurely wind blew through the trees, gently caressing the overhead branches of the pines that lined up our driveway. The air had warmed slightly since morning, making the outdoors a wonderful place to be right now. I didn't want to go inside, but I had to get the girls in bed. Sleep came quickly for me and the dreams stayed silent for the night—thank goodness.

Chapter Seven

The Court Date

I woke early and I stared out the window at the endless sky littered with clouds, some big and puffy, some thin and streaked, some resembling small animals. What a beautiful morning it was. I took a deep breath and enjoyed the moment. I was enjoying it too much because I jumped at the sound of the phone ringing.

"Hello?"

"Hi, Susan Green? It's John Wilson."

"Oh … Tina's lawyer." I rolled my eyes.

"How are you? I am calling to make sure you received the court date in the mail? Did you get the papers I sent you?" John asked.

"Yes, I did. Thank you," I replied.

I fidgeted about, walking around and trying to think of ways to end the call. I didn't have time for this. Not today, not really ever. I finally just told him I got them and I would be there and hung up the phone.

I then went to the girl's room. "Good morning, girls, time to wake up!" I announced as I entered their room, as I drew the curtains and allowed the bright sun to filter through the pink shades into their bedroom. They yawned and stretched their arms as I gave them a big smile. "What are we doing today, Grandma?" they asked sleepily.

"We have to get ready to go see Jackie, and then you have homework to do before dinner tonight." I was bustling about, folding their blankets and opening their closets to lay out clothes.

I shuffled the two of them into the bathroom to wash up. I went down to start breakfast while they got washed and dressed. "Good morning, my little ladies!" I greeted them again as they both walked into the kitchen. "Have your breakfast so we can go to Jackie's," I said cheerfully.

"Grandma, can we play outside today?" asked Amy.

"Of course you can if it gets warm enough. But hurry up and finish your breakfast so we can get to Jackie's house."

As we walked into Jackie's house, I could smell eggs frying. "Jackie, you promised you'd try to wait until I got here! You could have hurt yourself," I shouted out to her.

"I would have starved to death if I did," she shouted back at me.

She smiled as she said it so I knew she wasn't mad.

***

As the afternoon wore on, I cleaned and washed clothes for her as the girls played outside in the yard. The days went by so quickly, taking care of the girls and Jackie was making the time for court faster then I realized. Before I knew it, I was outside of a courthouse on the way to the custody hearing. As I walked down the never-ending hallway to the courtroom holding my granddaughters' hands, I saw Tina standing there with her lawyer.

"What are we doing here, Granny?" Kelly asked.

"I think the judge wants to know who you want to live with," I replied.

"Granny, Mommy is bad. She is mean to us!" Kelly replied.

"Just tell the judge who you want to be with and it will be ok," I told her.

By the time we entered the courthouse to take our seats, Tina was already seated next to her lawyer.

After the judge came in and asked Tina's lawyer to call his first witness, Tina was led to the podium by the bailiff. The lawyer started to interview her, and she calmly told him why I had the children and that she was better now and could take care of them. Without warning, Kelly ran up to the judge and started to hit him! She hit him as she screamed, "I want to live with my granny! I don't want my mom taking me away!" The judge called for a recess and we were hurriedly escorted out of the courtroom by my lawyer. I tried to calm Kelly down, but she was so upset. I should have prepared them for this, but I was scared and I really didn't know that they were going to make me bring them.

When the judge called us back in, they made me leave the girls with a social worker. *This day couldn't get any worse*, I thought. I was wrong. Even after my lawyer presented my evidence, the judge still ruled in her favor. She had won. I bolted out of my chair and ran through the halls toward where they had put the girls. There they stood, looking absolutely beautiful. My little angels. "Kelly, Amy! Come and say goodbye to grandma!" Those were the hardest words that ever came out of my mouth. "Kelly, do you know why you're here?" I asked.

"Yes, I do," she answered, looking down at the floor. "I'm here because Mommy wants us back."

"And how are you feeling now?"

"Very sad, Granny; I don't want to leave you," she cried.

"Honey I wish it could be different, but Granny has to do what the judge says and you have to go live with your mommy for a while. I will check on you as much as your mommy will let me, okay?" I tried my best to hold it together in front of the girls. The social worker came in and said it was time to go. I hugged them tight and whispered in their ears, "I will love you forever and I will always be in your heart when you need me. Just close your eyes and think of me and I will be there with you both." I had to let go and it broke my heart to walk away. Tears were burning my eyes as I stepped out of the room. Tina stood there looking at me with a smirk on her face. I looked at her and said, "Why would you do this to them?"

All she could say was, "They are my children, not yours."

I turned and walked out of my daughter's

life once more, but this time I lost everything I loved along with it, my beautiful grandchildren.

Part 2

Kelly's Story

Chapter Eight

A New, Confusing Life

"Kelly, Amy! Come and say hi to your mommy!" my mother said excitedly, like she was never gone from my life for all those years.

I ran over without any hesitation and gave her a hug. She lifted me up and hugged me back. I just knew right then and there that Mommy was going to be the best mommy ever.

It wasn't much longer than a few months when the fights between my mommy and her boyfriend began to get worse. She was being a good mommy at first. He would always end up walking out on her and staying away for days. I know they fought about money because I heard him say, "Stop spending my money on drugs". She accused him constantly of cheating on her with another woman.

One Wednesday afternoon, as I came home to get ready to do my homework, I rushed into my mother's bedroom to greet her. The air conditioner made a humming sound and the room was ice cold and eerily still. My mother had bad headaches, so the shades were pulled and the room was always black. "Mommy, I'm home. Are you sleeping again? I have to do my homework and I need help." I jumped on the bed like I'd become accustomed to, intending to take a short nap beside her. I reached out for her, but she wasn't on the bed. Just as I got up and headed out for the door, a feeling of dread washed over me. I felt a slight movement on the other side of the floor, so I climbed back on the bed and leaned over the edge to the opposite side. There, on the ground was my mother, slumped but alive, mumbling like she was drugged out of her mind. "Mommy, get up. What did you do? Did you fall? Where is Amy, Mommy?"

I went to look for Amy and I couldn't find her. I started to get scared. Then I heard a cry come from inside the closet. I opened the door to see my baby sister laying in wetness and crying. "How did you get in here, Amy?" I asked.

"Mommy locked me in here and told me to shut up," Amy replied.

I went back to Mommy's room to see if she was alright. As I entered the room, she was sitting on a chair. I wanted to ask my mommy about what had happened, but I didn't want to get her in a bad mood. She was very mean when she was mad at us. I took Amy into the kitchen after cleaning her up and asked her if she was hungry. She bit her bottom lip for a moment and looked at me like it was a very hard decision she had to make. Then she nodded. I made her a peanut butter sandwich. I was too young to make anything else. We both loved peanut butter, though.

Amy and I went to our room, and while I was doing my homework Amy played. "Quiet down, Amy. Mom's going to hear you," I mumbled. I didn't want to yell at Amy, but I didn't want Mommy to get mad. I threw my arms around her. I don't really know why, but she just seemed so sad all the time. I felt bad about yelling at her.

Sometimes I woke up in the morning and I had a weird feeling like I had a dream that I just couldn't remember. I would try really hard to think about it, but nothing was left of it in my head. It was just a feeling like something happened and I missed it. Some of my dreams were of my grandma and I really wanted to remember them. I really missed her waking us up each morning and fixing us breakfast. I went into my mother's room to see if she was awake. The room was empty so I headed for the living room. She was on the couch asleep. I really had to go to school, but I didn't want to leave Amy alone while she slept. I walked over quietly and shook her arm to try and wake her.

"What!?" she yelled, I told her I had to go to school and she needed to watch Amy. "Just go; I got Amy. I am her mother, you know!" she replied.

I just wanted to be invisible. I wanted to disappear forever. No one would care, I thought.

My mom nodded, got up, and left to go to the bathroom, and I got ready for school. But I just couldn't stop thinking about it. Why was she so mean now? Why did she hate us so much? I got yelled at by my teacher two times at school today for not paying attention. All I could think about was Amy. I hoped Mommy was taking care of her. She was supposed to be in school, too, but Mommy said she really didn't have to go to so she wasn't sending her. My lunch gave me a stomachache, too. I put a peanut butter sandwich in a bag for my lunch. I think I was eating too much peanut butter. Grandma always told me if I eat too much peanut butter I wouldn't be able to use the bathroom. I think she was right. I wanted to go home to grandma so bad.

Amy was already sitting on the floor when I got home from school. She seemed to be working very hard at figuring something out. "What do you have, Amy?" I asked. I walked over and looked down at the needle she held in her hand. I took it from her and asked where she got it.

"Mommy's room," she said. I could feel the jagged edges of the needle pressing into my hand. I put it in the trash can beside the couch. I checked Amy's hands to make sure she wasn't cut anywhere.

"Where is Mommy?" I asked her.

"In her room."

I walked to the room; it was dark as always. I could see her sitting in the chair beside her bed. I asked her if she was alright. She didn't answer me so I left to go see if Amy had eaten today. Of course she hadn't, so I looked through the cabinets to find something for us to eat. I found some canned fruit, but I didn't know how to use the can opener. I found some ham in the refrigerator and we ate that.

I went in the bathroom to get Amy cleaned up as much as I knew how to. I put clean clothes on her to sleep in and I read her one of my little books. "Hey! What is that?" Amy asked, looking at the pictures. It was a snail crawling along the side walk. She laughed and said that was a funny name.

"Yes." I laughed as I dropped down to the floor next to her. Our bed laid on the floor because Amy was jumping on it one day and broke it. Mommy said she wouldn't fix it because we had to learn to take care of our stuff. Sleep came fast for both of us.

Chapter Nine

He Returns!

Today was Friday and I was supposed to go to school but I overslept. The house was so quiet when I got up. I didn't know if Mommy was awake or not. Amy was still asleep, so I walked into the living room to see if she was in there. The room was dark as her bedroom always was; there was no sign of her in there. I went and looked all over the house, but she was not there. We were all by ourselves in the house. My life was seriously terrible. It might be the worst life ever. That may seem hard for most people to believe from an eight year old, but most people did not live my life. I considered just getting Amy and running away to Grandma's house, but I didn't know where it was. When Mommy brought us here, I had fallen asleep in the car. I went and sat on the couch to watch television while Amy slept. Suddenly, he touched my hair and twisted it around his finger a little. I jumped and screamed, which yanked my hair and I sort of fell over.

"I'm sorry! I'm so sorry! I didn't mean to scare you or pull your hair!" he said with such a worried look on his face. Where did he come from?

I didn't see anyone in the house. It was my mommy's boyfriend, Brad.

"When did you get back?" I asked.

"Just now," he replied.

I was so happy to see him. I threw my arms around his neck and hugged him so tight. Now there was someone there to take care of us. I hoped, anyway. I asked him where Mommy was. He said she went to the store. This was the first time she had been out since he left. He asked me if I had been going to school. I told him yes and I walked home every day and took care of Amy.

"Your mom lets you walk home alone?"

"Yeah, it is only a little more than three blocks away and she's usually sleeping or doing something else." I couldn't help but say what I was thinking because Grandma always told us to say what we were thinking, as long as it was the truth. The look in his eyes told me he was angry because I was walking home alone. I hoped I didn't cause them to fight again. Maybe I should have kept my mouth shut.

Mommy came back with bags of food. It all looked so good and my stomach growled. We didn't get to eat much while Brad was gone. I really hoped he stayed this time. I helped Mommy put the food away and then I asked her if she wanted me to help her make dinner. She smiled at me for the first time in a long time. It felt very nice to have her smile at me. She said yes with a loving pat on my back. The evening went really well. Everyone got along and even laughed and played around after dinner. Why couldn't it be this way all the time? I helped Amy get ready for bed while Mommy and John went to talk outside. I loved brushing her long blonde hair; it was so beautiful. I wished I had blonde hair, but I got Mommy's brown hair. Sleep came quick for me. I was so tired and having a full stomach helped, too.

***

The sun from the window woke me early. It was so bright outside today. Maybe this was a sign that things would be brighter in our lives. I sat up and looked to see if Amy was up yet, but she was still snuggled under her blanket. I could smell bacon frying and my stomach started to growl. I got up and dressed and went to the kitchen to find Brad fixing breakfast for everyone. I loved it when he cooked; his food tasted so good.

"Where is Mommy?" I asked him.

"She is still asleep. I didn't want to wake her until I had this done."

I could hardly wait to taste that bacon and

eggs. I heard footsteps coming toward the kitchen and I turned to see if it was Amy, but it was Mommy rubbing her eyes to help them adjust to the light. "Good morning," I said.

She looked at me like I had just cursed her. "What is so good about it?" she said. I clammed up right then, knowing she was not in a good mood today. Brad told her to go back and lay down and he would bring her food to her, but she got mad about it and said, "If I can't sit in here with you guys and eat then no one eats."

I couldn't believe what she did next.

Food went flying everywhere as she was grabbing it and tossing it to the floor. She screamed when she grabbed the hot pan and burned her hand really bad. Brad stopped her from throwing the pan at me. I ran to my room and closed the door, hoping Brad could calm her down. Amy woke up as I closed the door and asked me if it was time to eat. I told her no not yet and she lay back down. I was hoping she would fall back to sleep so she wouldn't hear them arguing down the hall. It seemed like hours before Brad finally came into the room and told us we could come eat now. Mommy had gone back to her room. Brad had cleaned up the mess and cooked us more food. I could not understand what made her so mad. I sat there eating, wanting to ask Brad what was wrong with

Mommy, but I was afraid to say anything. So I just finished my breakfast and asked to be excused from the table. Grandma always told us to ask to leave the table before we got up. Brad just nodded his head and then lowered it back down toward the table. Amy just sat there eating everything in sight.

I wished I could talk to Brad and see if he would take us to see Grandma for a while. I missed her so much and I knew she wanted to see us, too. Maybe I could catch Mommy gone one day and see if he would do that for us. I hoped he would. I wanted to hug my nana again.

The day went by fast. Amy and I stayed away from the other side of the house so we wouldn't bother Mommy. We played in our room and went out back for a little while. She never came out of her room that day, not even for dinner. I guess it was just one of her bad days.

Morning came quick and I woke to the front door slamming. I walked into the living room to see Brad sitting on the chair. "Where is Mommy?" I asked.

"She went shopping," he replied. I thought this would be a good time to ask him about going to see Grandma.

"What do you need to know?" Brad knew I wanted something.

"Can you take us to see Grandma without

Mommy knowing? It's a secret," I whispered.

He looked at me and smirked. "So this will be our little secret from your Mom, huh? I will try and see what I can do, but no promises, okay?" he said. I was so excited just to hear him say he would try. He reached into his pocket. "I found it in your mom's room. It was shiny and beautiful. I grabbed it for you. I know how important it is to you. It was your grandmother's right?" He passed it to me. I put it on and tried to ignore that it slid on too easily. It was too big. It was grandma's charm bracelet she had made after she got Amy and me. It has our birthstones in it. She wore it all the time. I don't know how mommy got it, but I was glad to have it back.

I blushed. "How do you know it's important to me?"

He shrugged. "I pay more attention than you'd imagine, Kelly."

I really liked Brad! He was so good to us and he took care of everything that Mom didn't. I really hoped he could take us to see Grandma. I wasn't going to tell Amy yet just in case we didn't get to go. I didn't want her to be heartbroken if we didn't go. Mom returned from her shopping, but she didn't have any bags with her. I wondered what she had bought. Brad didn't say much to her as she walked right passed us and went to her room. She yelled back at Brad, asking what he was cooking for lunch. He didn't answer; just got up and went to the kitchen. I went in to check on Amy as he cooked.

Then I noticed the absence of noise, which was unusual when it came to my sister. She wasn't there so I walked to the front door. I stepped outside and stood on the front porch. I went back inside and headed up the stairs toward my bedroom and saw my closed bedroom door. Stopping in front of it, I hesitated, then turned the knob and pushed the door open. When I saw what was inside, my mouth fell open, my heart dropped to my stomach, and I felt my knees go weak. Amy had another needle and was playing with it. I ran over to her and took it from her and yelled at her to never touch these again. She started crying and I felt so bad I just hugged her tight. She must have sneaked into Mom's room again. I had to watch her closer from now on. Amy's face lit up with a warm smile. "Yeah I will never do it again...we're sisters, right?" All I could do was smile back at her and nod my head yes. I took her downstairs so we could eat lunch with Brad and maybe Mom.

Amy sat on her side of the table right next to our mom, who was slumped over and high again. Brad prepared their lunch, another can of beans and corn bread. Brad didn't say anything. He worried constantly about the situation and that worrying had only intensified with Mom's worsening addiction. Mom fills four spoons with a heap of beans. "We been thinking," she begins. Brad's jaw tightens as he takes his spoonful of food. "How would you girls like to go to a party with us?" I really didn't want to go so I didn't answer her.

Brad swallowed his beans and then spoke up. "Don't you see the girls don't want to go? Leave it alone."

Mom ignored Brad. "Why don't you think it over? No rush..."

I nodded slowly. "Okay..."

I really didn't want to go with them, but I knew if I said no she would be very angry with me. I sat and ate in silence while they talked about the party. Mom seemed really excited about it, but Brad acted like he didn't want to go either. Amy didn't say a word the whole time; she just sat and ate her lunch. I knew as soon as I was done she would ask me what I had decided, so I took my time eating. Hoping she would leave the table before me. That didn't happen.

She waited until I was finished and asked me. "Have you made up your mind yet Kelly?" I told her that her and Brad could go and I would watch Amy.

Brad spoke up right away and said, "I don't think you are old enough to watch Amy all by yourself so we all will stay home tonight."

That didn't go very well with Mom; she was very angry now.

"What the hell?" she mumbled. "I want to go," she said.

"Then go without me," Brad replied

"Fine." She sighed. "I'm going to grab a beer. Want anything?"

Brad shook his head, eyes focused on his plate. Brad never heard the footsteps until Tina was right on top of him. He was in the middle of turning around to find the source of the noise when she grabbed his shirt and thrust him, face first, into the kitchen wall. "Oooff. What the fuck..." Brad began to say, but was stopped short when she thrust him into the wall again.

"Shut your mouth, you sick bastard," Mom spat in his ear. She turned him around, harder than necessary. Brad's eyes were wide and his lip was bleeding, a result of the fresh cut born of skin being introduced to the hard wall. They stared at each other for a stretch of time before the fright in Brad's eyes was replaced by anger.

Brad's eyes doubled in size as he grabbed my mother by the hair, pulling her into the other room. But Mom didn't notice the shock in them. She was too far gone into her own angry-induced madness to notice much of anything outside of her own head. "It was a fucking accident!" She was openly crying now. "It just came out of nowhere. I was mad because you were not going. I had one too many beers. I didn't mean it..." Sobs cut off any further attempts at speaking.

"What did I do? What did I do? What did I do?" Brad repeated the phrase over and over again to himself, his voice echoing off every surface of the living room. "I am sorry, Tina. I can't do this anymore!" he said.

I started to cry as he walked out the door. I knew it would be the last time we would see him, and my chances of seeing Grandma had plummeted.

Chapter Ten

Now it gets bad!

Later that night, I was lying in bed, tossing and turning because I couldn't sleep. Eventually, I gave up and put my clothes and shoes on and climbed out my window. I needed fresh air and I really didn't want to be in that house anymore. I looked down the driveway and saw that my mother's car was not there. When had she left? I climbed back into my room and went down to her room. It was dark as always, but this time she was not in there. She must have went to the party after all. I went to the living room to watch television for a little while. I fell asleep as soon as I laid on the couch.

***

When I woke Amy was sitting below me watching her favorite show. I asked her where Mom was, but she didn't know. I went to check her room, but it was still dark and empty. I went to the kitchen to make us something to eat. I couldn't cook so I had to find something to eat that didn't need to be fixed and most of the time it was peanut butter and jelly.

The day went by fast as we played outside and then came in for dinner with no signs of my mother returning. I cleaned Amy up as well as I could and got her ready for bed. I was hoping that my mother would return tonight so I could go to school tomorrow.

The time grew later and later and there was no signs of her retuning. I went upstairs to lay down in my room, but sleep would not come. All I could do was think about going back to Grandma's house and have the chance at happiness again. Thinking about the times she would play with us and fix us treats and just love us. Would we ever have that in our lives again? I sat and thought what if Mom changed and she started to love us again, like a mother should. How wonderful it would be to have a mom who cared and wanted us around. I wanted that so bad, but I didn't see it happening. I didn't know what to do to make her like us again.

***

The next day, Mom returned for a short time. She told me she would be gone for a while, but she would check in on us. During the time she would be gone, my mother left me a huge list of jobs that I needed to have completed by the time she got home. She also swore that she was going to drop by randomly to check on me and alluded to having some sort of surveillance set up to make sure I stayed home and took care of Amy. She brought a few groceries that I could fix for us and she said I was not to answer the door at all while she was gone. I asked her when she would be back and all she could say was, "When I walk through the door, you will know I am back."

***

A few weeks passed after Mom left and things were starting to settle down at home. I spent quite a bit of my free time with Amy. She was so sweet and so lovable and aside from an occasional mild temper tantrum and her lower birth weight, we didn't see any serious side effects of my mother's drug dependency while she was pregnant. We were told to expect some learning disabilities along the way, but so far Amy seemed to be focused and alert. Our home life was often tense and stressful. My mother was always on edge when she returned for her short visits, trying to please the new man in her life. He had a wife and family who often called our house to harass her and to demand that she send him back home to them. When they would do that, she would disappear once again for days at a time. The school never called so I guessed Mom had told them some lie for the reason I hadn't been to school.

***

A few more weeks passed and life was uneventful. I was focused on spending time with Amy, and my mother was either sleeping a lot or out with her friends. There were daily fights and emotional screaming matches between her and her boyfriend. Nothing new. Same old routine again. I had taken to becoming the mother of the house, cleaning and cooking, giving instructions for Amy, while my mother slept through it all. When she was awake and lucid, she was always in and out. But she was also moody and delusional, often telling us that she could spend all she wanted, knowing that her boyfriend would bail her out of any financial bind. She also had a crying fit when she found out that Brad's new wife had given birth to a son.

One day she was gone and her boyfriend came to the door and I knew I wasn't supposed to answer the door, but I saw it was him and I didn't want her to get mad at me for not answering so I let him in. He walked in and asked where my mother was. I told him I didn't know. He asked me to get him something to drink so I did. When I returned with the drink, he was all over me. Me, an 8 year old. Why would he do this? He told me to take off my clothes and I was scared not to. Not knowing what he would do, I was shaking as I pulled off my shirt, unbuttoned my jeans, and stepped out in just my bra and panties.

"I love you, Kelly," he said, as I stood in front of him. He didn't even know me. "You are the most beautiful girl I have ever seen," he said as he unclasped my bra and pulled my panties down. I was completely naked. He touched me all over and squeezed my breasts as they barely laid in his hands. "I love your breasts, Kelly. Let me taste them." He tugged at my nipples as he pressed himself against me even more. I knew this was wrong, but I didn't know how to get him to stop. As he was getting ready to pull his pants down, my mother walked in and she started hitting me. Calling me a whore and hitting me over and over again. All I could do was put my hands up and protect myself from the blows of her fist.

That night, I was lying in bed, worried and confused about what happened. Why did she blame me for what he did to me? Did I do something wrong to make him do that to me? Maybe I was just a bad girl who didn't deserve to be loved by anyone at all. I laid there and cried myself to sleep. Dreams came as soon as I shut my eyes. I could see my grandmother saying, "Child, just close your eyes and I will be with you." She stood there with her arms open like she was waiting on me to run to her, but I couldn't move. It was like I was frozen to the ground. I started screaming her name and the tears fell to my cheeks. She had tears in her eyes also and I could feel her pain.

I woke from the dream with tears still in my eyes. Amy was lying next to me with her doll and she didn't even move as I slipped out of the bed. I was hoping that my mom was not home. I didn't know if she was still mad at me or not and what she would do to me if she was. I went to the living room to see if she was there, but she wasn't. So I quietly went to her room and opened the door. It was dark and there were no signs of her. I was relieved that she was gone, for now anyway. I did my normal routine of fixing something to eat for Amy and we played in our room for the rest of the day until that evening. That evening, my mother walked in from the rain as Amy and I sat in the living room to wait for her. Amy paced back and forth as we heard the car enter the driveway. She walked in, looking rested and refreshed. She didn't look mad anymore so that was a relief to me.

***

The next few days and months flew by in a blur. Mom stayed gone a lot and I was in charge of Amy. I wanted to go back to school so badly. Mom hadn't been home in days, and one night Amy was sick and running a fever. I didn't know what to do for her and I knew I was not to call anyone or she

101

would beat me again. I remembered Grandma putting me in a cold bath when I was sick so I did that and it helped for a little while, but the fever came back hours later. I was getting scared and didn't know what else to do. I lay with her, praying it would go away. I thought to myself what if I could find Grandma's house and take her there, she would know how to take care of her. I didn't know if I could find it, though.

I had to try so I got her dressed and put her shoes on and then dressed myself. We started out the door to head to Grandma's house. I didn't know how to get there, but I was going to try and find her know matter what.

Chapter Eleven

To Grandma's house we go!

It was very dark outside with the moon glowing overhead. Amy asked me where we were going and I told her to Grandma's house. "She will take care of you."

It seemed like we walked miles when we came up to this house with lights on. I told Amy I would ask the people here if they knew where Grandma lived. I knew her real name; I just didn't know the street name where she lived. The house was a big brick house with flowers all around it. There was music playing inside so I hoped they would hear me knock. I knocked as hard as I could with my small hands. No one came to the door. We stood there for a very long time, waiting to see if someone would come out. After a while, Amy started to cry while saying she didn't feel well at all. I was so scared and I didn't know what to do.

I banged on the door again and again and still no answer came. I told Amy that we had to continue to walk to Grandma's house. She didn't want to walk anymore, but she did. I had no idea where I was going and it was getting later and later. The night air was getting colder and that helped bring her fever down some. We were so tired, but we had to continue on our journey to get to Grandma's house. There wasn't a lot of cars on the road at that time of night so we walked on the road mostly. The pavement was easier to walk on than the dirt beside the road.

Amy had to stop walking, so I found a tree and let her lay against it to rest for a while. I sat beside her and rested my head against hers. We were asleep before I blinked. I woke to the screams of a woman who had a very angry voice. The voice of my mother. She had found us and now she was madder than a hornet. She jerked Amy up and put her in the car and grabbed me by the arm and pushed me in the car, too. I tried to explain to her that Amy was sick and I didn't know what to do because she wasn't there to help me. She did not reply to anything I said, so I sat there quietly until we got home. She took Amy upstairs to our room and gave her something and put her to bed. Then she came downstairs to talk to me.

"Where were you going?" she asked.

I didn't know if I should tell her or not, but I knew if I didn't say something she would hit me again.

"I was taking Amy to Grandma's house so she could get her better."

"Grandma's," she replied. "Your grandmother is dead!" she yelled.

"No!" I screamed.

"She died in a car accident a month ago, Girl!"

The tears started running down my face. My grandma couldn't be dead. She had to come get us and take care of us again. What were we going to do now? I didn't want to stay in the same room with her any longer so I ran to my room and closed the door behind me. This couldn't be happening; she couldn't be dead. What would our lives be like now? What if something happened to Mom; who would take care of us? I didn't want to be here anymore, but I didn't want to leave Amy.

I stayed in my room until I thought Mom had time to calm down and I went downstairs to get Amy something to eat and drink. It was quiet and the house was dark. Maybe she had left again. I was hoping that she had. I went into the kitchen and she was at the table sitting there with her head laying on the table. "Mom," I said carefully. She didn't answer me. I went over to her and shook her shoulder. Nothing. She was passed out at the table. I got something to drink and eat and went back to my room. She had done this a million times, so I was not worried that she was dead or anything. Amy's fever was gone. I didn't know what she gave her, but it helped her. She was sitting up in the bed when I came back. She asked me what was wrong and I told her that Grandma had died. She started crying and I held her and told her it would be okay; she still had me.

She got up and headed to the bathroom to take a bath. I waited outside for her, but when she took so long I went in to check on her. Amy stepped out of the shower and wrapped a fluffy white towel around her body. She cleared the steam from the mirror and inspected her nose, which was no longer red. She squinted her eyes, scrunched her mouth, and moved her lips from side to side. She puckered, as if to kiss someone, and I couldn't help but laugh at her. She looked like she was feeling a lot better now.

Her hair was a mass of fuzz, with no way to tame it in sight. There was nothing she could do about that; she was born with hair like our father's, but on steroids. Our father's hair was coarse, like hers, with tight, little, perfectly formed curls. The kink and curls of her thick, blonde hair were so different from mine and Mother's straight, brown hair that she always felt a bit like an alien in her own family.It was almost midnight when Amy finally hugged me one last time and told me goodnight. I loved my sister so much and without her I wouldn't want to live.

***

The next few weeks were kind of good. Mom had met a new man and she was in love. He seemed real nice, but I really didn't know because we didn't get to spend a lot of time with him. After our mother remarried, we moved into a dusty, blue and black house on the north side of town. We were excited to live in a new house and change schools, and felt lucky that there were new friends to be made in the green house right next door. Carrie, who was about ten, twelve-year-old Sammie, and fifteen-year-old, Linda. They marveled about the two of us being identical in every way, from the moles on our left cheeks to our tomboyish fondness for climbing trees. Whenever our mother came home from friends' houses and didn't see us jumping rope outside, hanging around the kitchen, or watching television, she knew we'd be playing near the swings in our neighbor's backyard or inside their house. We played games with all our new friends, solved jigsaw puzzles, or polished our fingernails with Cassie, and ate up the food their mother, Ann, cooked for us.

Life was good and I hoped it would stay that

way. It was raining hard. At first there was only a sprinkle, then lightning flashed, and a downpour of rain beat against the roof. We sat in our neighbors' living room and debated whether or not we should run through the thunderstorm to our house, but the good smells that came from Ann's kitchen made our mouths water. We stayed put. A pot clanged on the burner. We went in to inspect.

"Melt the butter to mix with the herbs," Ann said to Cassie, who stopped what she was doing to retrieve the butter from the refrigerator.

Ann was tall and fine-boned, with large doe-eyes framed by long lashes. She moved about the one-story house with a self-possessed grace in her pink dress. We thought she would make a good model. She could sell anything but perfume, because she always had a smell: parsley, cilantro, chicken, goat, sour soup, shop cheese. She was her stepmother's helper chef; she cut vegetables, strained rice, stirred sugar into a mug full of milk, shelled peas, and completed chores around the house before she started her homework.

Our mother hadn't taught us much about cooking. She said she preferred us to stay out of the kitchen so we wouldn't drop anything or make a mess. But we knew it was mostly because she hardly ever cooked. But I wasn't going to tell our new friends about our lives behind closed doors.

Mom came over to get us and I knew something was wrong by the look on her face. I was watching her walk out and as she did her shirt fell down some of her shoulder, exposing a red mark on her shoulder, and she hurriedly adjusted it, glancing at us sideways. The red mark made us watch her more closely. There was something different about her today. She seemed to be like her old self again, the mean self.

***After the rain stopped that night and the full moon came out, we fell asleep praying for her happiness. When I got home from school the next afternoon, our stepfather was there, having worked a half-day. "We're going fishing at the lake when homework is done," he said.

Excited to fish, I hurried through my assignments, multiplication problems, vocabulary words, fill-in-the-blank sentences about stupid stuff. Then we piled into the back of his car. We really wanted to catch some fish this time, imagining the trout we were going to catch at the lake, already seeing the salt and pepper that our step-father would shake onto each fish before he threw them into the hot pan of bubbling oil. The car moved slowly down the dusty hill, past younger children playing at the side of the road by parked vehicles. That's when we saw it; a bruise on the back of my mother's neck. Had my step-dad been hitting her? It had to be him. Who else would do that to her? All I could think at that moment was here we go again. Life could not stay good for us for very long.

He seemed to be a very nice man. He stood six feet tall and was on the heavy side with brown hair and brown eyes. He was very kind to us girls. I didn't understand how anyone could hit another person. It saddened my heart. The marriage happened so fast, though. Did we really know him? I was going to watch and see what happened next. I hoped our world didn't turn upside down again. I was back in school and I had friends now. I loved our new friends, but I still wouldn't tell them about our lives. The only thing I had told them was about my grandma dying and how wonderful she was. The day fishing was nice, but Mom just sat under a tree the whole time and didn't talk to anyone. I knew something wasn't right, but I just didn't know what it was yet. We left the lake at dark and by the time we got home it was late. Amy and I went to our room to get ready for bed. I was brushing Amy's hair when I heard a lot screams coming from down the hall.

It was Mom screaming, I ran down the hall to see her laying on the floor with blood coming from her mouth. Paul had hit her in the face and knocked her down. I started yelling. "Leave my mom alone!"

He turned to me and told me to go back to my room or I would get the same. I didn't want to leave her, but I knew if he hit me like that he would hurt me bad. So I ran back to my room crying. I didn't know what to do to help her. I could hear them yelling back and forth at each other.

Amy asked me what was going on and I just told her they were arguing, but it would be okay. She didn't need to know anything else right now. God, would our lives ever get better? I helped Amy get ready for bed. When it finally got quiet, I walked down the hall to see if I could see my mom anywhere. She was nowhere to be found. I saw Paul in the chair and asked him where my mom was and all he could say was she went out. I went back to my room and laid down. Sleep took forever to arrive that night.

***

February came quickly, and with it, came the cold weather, as well as my birthday. I was one of the rare people who was born on the 29th of the month, so for a long time Grandma had just celebrated my birthday on the last day of the month, and we'd have a party every leap year for my actual birth date. We were currently in a leap year and after all the drama I'd been through at home, the last thing I wanted was to invite them all to a party. All I wanted was the day off school, so I could go spend it with Amy. A few people remembered that there should have been a party and asked me about it, but most of them didn't even know.

Amy hugged me as soon as she opened her eyes and said, "Happy Birthday!" I loosened my arms, so she could step away from me, and I could see her face. She had her lips pressed together in a smile, and she wiped at her eyes while trying not to meet mine.

"Hey? Why are you getting upset?" I asked, furrowing my brow in concern as I peered into her face.

"It's the first birthday without Grandma," she replied.

That made the tears fall from my eyes as well.

"I'm sorry. I wasn't trying to upset you. I think about her all the time," Amy said.

I think about her every day that goes by and I wish she was alive and for us to be able to live with her again. I knew Mom wouldn't remember my birthday and I wasn't about to mention it to Paul. It was just another day, anyway. Amy and I dressed and went to the house next door for a little while. Mom was still not home and Paul was at work. I had the day off of school and I wasn't going to sit in that house all day by ourselves.

***

I had been over at Ann's house watching movies with everyone all day and when I came home, there was another car parked in our driveway. It looked fairly new, and I quickened my pace to find out who was visiting. When I walked in the door, I could only find my mother in the kitchen doing something at the table.

"Who's here?" I asked her straight away.

"Well, hello to you, too."

"Sorry, Mom—Hi. Whose car is outside?"

"Mine."

"Are you serious?"

"I sure am."

"Mom! Please don't take this the wrong way, but how did you get the money for a car like that? I don't want to sound disrespectful, but if you're in debt for it, Paul might get mad."

She smiled gently at me. "You're very sweet to worry about the cost and that Paul might not like it, but I do what I want, too. But I assure you. I am not in debt one bit. It's all mine, and it's all paid for."

***

We went driving for maybe an hour, talking and listening to music. It felt great to have some time with Mom alone, and I was on a high for the rest of the afternoon. When I got home, Paul was there and he told me to go next door with my sister and that he and Mom had to talk. I hoped that was all they were going to do. I couldn't stand him any more since he hit my mom. I left, not really wanting to, but I knew if I didn't it would be worse. But I didn't stay long over there.

Chapter Eleven

The truth comes out!

I stood up and listened at the door, their voices becoming too low for me to hear. I ventured out of my room to make sure everything was alright. "Mom?" I called. "What's going on?"

"Nothing, Kelly. Just go back to bed. Don't you dare take that car, Paul!" she yelled, chasing my step-father out the door.

Balling my hands into fists, I stormed toward the door and grabbed the metal baseball bat we had sitting there in case the wrong kind of person came to our door. By the time I got outside, he was already in the driver's seat of the car. All the pain that I had felt had been replaced by the anger and hatred I felt toward the man who was currently taking it from my mom. The man who hit my mom. Before he could put the car in gear, I swung the bat, bringing it down on the windshield with all the strength I could muster. I heard a loud crack as the glass splintered in a jagged pattern.

I swung the bat again, this time taking off the side mirror with a clean swipe, causing the mirror to shatter, spraying glass up the concrete driveway. He reversed the car as fast as he could, screeching the tires as he straightened himself on the road. All the while, I was chasing him down the drive, beating on the car and denting the panels until he started to drive off. Then with strength born of rage, frustration, and hate, I hurled the baseball bat at the back window, causing it to pop through the glass and lodge itself inside.

"I hate you!" I screamed after him, standing in the middle of the road with no shoes on and glass around my feet as I watched him drive away in my mom's car. At least I got to see him leave— hopefully for good.

"Oh Kelly," my mother said, her hand covering her mouth as tears threatened to spill from her eyes. "You are your mother's daughter."

Instead of talking to her, I ran. I was so keyed up that I didn't even notice the pain of the asphalt road on the bottom of my bare feet. I ran straight to the one person I always thought of when something was happening in my life. I ran to Amy.

"Oh my god, what's happened?" she asked immediately as she opened the bedroom door. I suddenly realized that not only was I shoeless, but I was bleeding as well; standing outside our bedroom door and bleeding everywhere

116

"Our step-dad," was all I could say. Her face fell as she quickly grabbed my arm and helped me inside.

"Oh Kelly, your feet!" she gasped, looking down at them. "Stay there, I'll be right back."

I dropped onto her desk chair with a thud and finally looked at my feet. They were filthy and bleeding from the glass and jagged road I ran along. I wasn't angry at my mom at all. I just didn't want to talk about what happened with her yet. Right now, I needed Amy.

Amy returned to the room with an old towel, a bowl of water, and a first-aid kit. She knelt down in front of me and laid the towel on the floor under my feet and started to gently clean them for me, inspecting my cuts for pieces of glass and debris before applying antiseptic and bandages. I sat quietly and watched her work, fighting my tears the entire time. She was so young, but she seemed to know what she was doing. "Are you going to tell me what happened?" she asked. "It's okay to cry, Kelly. It's me. It's not like I'm going to tell anyone," she whispered, rising up on her knees and wrapping her arms around me. "It's okay." I leaned into her and let go, crying like a baby. If anyone else had been there, I would have been so embarrassed. But it was just Amy and me, and this was the first time I ever let the fact that my step-father was hitting my mom come out. I wasn't upset over the car. I really didn't care if she had a new car or not. It was just that she was happy and now she was not. When she was not happy, we were not happy.

Eventually, we lay down on her bed together, and I told her everything about how he had hit Mom and I thought it had been going on for a while now. She listened quietly and held me, gently stroking my hair as I spoke. I don't remember at what point we fell asleep, but when I woke up, my head was on her chest and her arms were still wrapped around me. When I opened my eyes, sore and swollen from a night of being upset, it took a while for me to focus and realize that the door to our room was open. In the doorway stood Mom, leaning against the frame with her arms crossed and a very unimpressed look on her face.

Amy stirred. "What?" she asked, her voice heavy with sleep as she rubbed her eyes to get her focus. Suddenly, she sat upright with a gasp. "Mom!" I swung my legs out of the bed and went to stand, pain shooting through my feet as I took my weight.

"Crap," I hissed.

She looked like she was mad, but I didn't know why she would be mad at me. I was just trying to help her. She told me to watch Amy because she would be leaving for a few days. *No school again*, I thought. I couldn't say no, as much as I wanted to. Amy started school next month so at least then I would be able to go every day. I would just have to catch up on everything once again. We cut ourselves off and quit going next door all together. We just couldn't be bothered anymore. We had to keep our life a secret from everyone. My only worry was that Paul would come back and beat me half to death. I didn't answer the door at all and we stayed inside the whole time Mom was gone. It was like being in jail, even though I didn't know what that felt like. I did watch a lot of crime shows. Amy slept a lot and played in her room while I took care of the house and her. The days seemed long and boring. I wished Mom would come home.

***

I put Amy on the school bus the next day. It was her first day of 1ˢᵗ grade. Then deciding it might not be such a great idea to stick around the neighborhood interviewing the neighbors— neighbors I'd never bothered getting to know really well—I walked as fast as I could, which wasn't very fast with the heavy backpack on my shoulders, and headed away from my house. As I passed the path I had taken the days before, I stared down the wooded trail, but kept on walking, heading for the main road. Five minutes later, I reached the road and considered hitchhiking into town instead of going to school. Maybe in town I could find out what had happened to my mom. I walked along the road, waiting for a car to come by so I could try to get a ride. No cars came and I kept walking, thinking about the strange things that were happening. I tried convincing myself that this was just a nightmare and that I was asleep. I pinched my arm, hard, hoping I would wake up, but the only thing that happened was a sharp pain in my arm that was sure to leave a bruise. Tears of frustration filled my eyes. I thought about my mom. I would do anything to find her. Then I frowned at the irony. Yesterday I had been so mad at Mom that I couldn't wait to run away from home. Today I was devastated that I couldn't be with her. I even missed Amy already and I had just left her. Trudging along the road, I tried to think of a reason, any reason, why she hadn't returned yet. Nothing came to mind.

Finally, I came to a bus stop that had a bench and a wooden structure shading it, probably built by some boy trying to earn his Eagle Scout award. That was fine with me. All I wanted was a place to stop and have something to eat. I dropped onto the bench, exhausted, and set the backpack on the seat next to me. I nibbled on some dried fruit, and then drank some water. After my hunger was partially satisfied, I reached into a side pocket and pulled out a small notebook along with a pen. My hand trembled as I set the small notepad on my lap. I clutched the pen in my other hand until the shaking stopped, then forced myself to write. **My name is Kelly Green. I'm nine years old and I don't understand what is happening.** I set the pen down and stared at the empty street, slouching on the bench, wondering if a bus would actually be coming. Fresh confusion swept over me and I gnawed on the inside of my lip. What was happening? Where was my mom? Squeezing my eyes closed, I tried to make sense of the last few days, but nothing made sense.

Trying to focus my thoughts on something constructive to do, I decided to write down the steps I could take to find my mom. Trying to distract myself from the bizarre errand I was now on, I concentrated on using my best penmanship. **Find a computer and Google her.** I stared at what I'd written. "It's not much of a list," I murmured. Pen poised over the paper, I had no idea what else to write.

The rumble of a bus saved me from thinking too hard about my situation. Quickly stuffing my notebook and pen into the side pocket of my backpack, I pulled out my wallet. The door to the bus whooshed open and I climbed the steps, stopping next to the bus driver. "How much to ride the bus?" I asked.

He barely glanced my way. "Two dollars." Unzipping the compartment on my wallet where I kept the bills, I frowned as I looked inside. I was living off the cash I'd had in my wallet and I didn't have a penny over thirty dollars. Ann had made sure she paid me for helping her with some stuff around her house. The bus driver cleared his throat and threw a look my way. Frowning, I dug out two dollars and shoved them into the receptacle then turned toward the seats. There were only a handful of people on the bus. I sat in the first empty seat, which was in the front row, but not the one behind the bus driver. I never liked to sit right behind the bus driver; I always felt like I was being watched when I sat there. He pulled the handle to close the door and we lumbered down the road. I knew it would take at least ten minutes to reach town, having driven there with my mom a few times. I watched the blur of trees as we sped past the forest. The trees changed to meadows and I stared at the few houses we passed, wondering if my mom could be in one of them.

When the bus stopped in the center of town, I climbed off, dragging my backpack with me. I headed down the main street, on the lookout for a place to use a computer. Starting off in a random direction, I looked at the store fronts as I passed. Boutiques, bookstores, and mom and pop diners lined the road. Nothing with public access to a computer. But then it occurred to me that one of the stores might have a phone book, which would also have the information I needed. A few minutes later, I found myself standing in front of the *Come on Inn Diner*. It looked like they had rooms available above the diner, which must be where the Inn part of the name came from. I opened the door and the smell of hamburgers wafted toward me, making my stomach growl. Ignoring my first impulse to go right to the counter, I made my way to the ladies room and pushed through the door. I saw two stalls, but both were unoccupied. Glad to be alone, I went to the sink and looked at myself in the mirror. Normally I kept my wavy, dark hair under control, but now it stuck up in several places. Plus, my face needed washing. I set my backpack on the floor, and then splashed warm water on my face. I ran my wet hands through my hair, forcing it to behave. I grabbed a handful of paper towels and dried my face and hands, then used the damp paper towels to wipe the dirt off my shoes. Tossing the dirty paper towels in the trash, I looked in the mirror again and thought I looked presentable, even if I didn't look my best. Just then a woman walked in and went into a stall. I grabbed my backpack and left, heading directly toward the counter.

Sliding onto a stool, I picked up the menu, deciding I could take a moment to eat something before continuing my quest. The menu choices were a bit surprising: veggie burgers, low-fat soups and salads, low-calorie deli sandwiches. I'd never had a veggie burger before, but was too hungry to be picky and decided to order one with all the fixings, along with a diet soda. "What can I get you, Hon?" the waitress asked, her pencil at the ready on her notepad. I told her what I wanted and she didn't respond, but stared at me. Finally she said, "Don't you think you're a little young to be in here by yourself?" I told her I was waiting on my mother to get here and she wanted me go ahead and order. "The vegetable minestrone is especially good," she replied.

I felt my eyebrows furrow. "Is there something wrong with the veggie burger?"

"Oh no. It's fantastic." She smiled, showing straight white teeth framed by bright red lips.

"Then why would I want the soup?"

She glanced in the direction of my waist, then met my eyes. "Veggie burger it is."

When she turned around to give the order to the cook, I looked down at my stomach self-consciously and sat up straighter, sucking in my gut. That was twice today someone had suggested I needed to lose weight. I couldn't believe how rude some people were. A short time later, the waitress placed my order in front of me, a look of disapproval on her face. I almost said something rude to her, but instead asked if she had a phone book I could look through. A moment later, she placed one on the counter next to my plate and I eagerly flipped to the T's. Running my finger down the page, I saw there were a lot of people's names in there and I knew none of them. This was not going to help me find Mom.

I looked at my veggie burger and found my appetite had diminished. Knowing my funds were limited and that it might be a while before I had the chance to eat a hot meal, I forced myself to eat half of the burger and asked for a box to put the rest in. The waitress smiled with apparent approval that I hadn't eaten the whole thing and I decided I wouldn't leave her a tip. She placed an empty box next to my plate and turned away to refill a customer's coffee mug. There was no way I was fat as I never ate. I didn't understand people sometimes. I remembered my mom telling me about her dancing to make money sometimes, so I asked the waitress if she knew where there was a place where ladies dance for money.

She told me yes but said that was not a place for a young lady as myself. I lied and told her my mom worked there and I had to catch up with her. She pointed out the window in the general direction I had come from. "You go on down Main Street until you get to the *Green Leaf Bookstore*. Then you make a left and go two blocks. Then you take a right and go three blocks. There's a little park there and you'll find that street right by the park." I wrote furiously in my notebook, knowing there was no way I could remember the directions otherwise.

"Thank you." I placed the box with my leftover hamburger in my backpack for Amy. I had to make sure I got home in time for her.

The Blue Moon Pub wasn't far from the diner and I stopped in front of it, looking at the window display. My eyebrows went up in surprise at the titles shown in the window. **Go Go Dancers and More!** What did that mean? The place wasn't very big and it had a lot of lights in it and very loud music.

"Can I help you?" a woman asked.

I turned around and saw a slender woman with straight blond hair. Curious if my assumption was correct, I said, "Actually, I was wondering. Does Tina Green work here?" To my surprise, she said yes she does. I asked her if she was there now. She told me to come with her, but to close my eyes when we got in the big room. Of course I didn't and I couldn't believe my mother worked in a place like this one. There were naked ladies everywhere hanging all over men. The lady yelled at this other girl and asked if she had seen Tina. The young girl told us that she left for a fix about an hour ago.

"A fix? What's that?" I asked.

The blonde said nothing, but the younger one said, "Drugs, baby doll."

God, she was doing drugs just like Grandma said. I overheard Grandma and Jackie talking right before we had to leave her. This was why she was working in a place like this. I knew she was drinking, but I really thought she stopped doing the drugs. I had to get out of there before she spotted me. I asked the lady not to say anything about me being there today and she said she wouldn't.

Somehow I restrained myself and walked out. I headed back toward the main road until I was near the diner again, then began following the directions the waitress had given me to get to *The Lazy Inn Pub* and followed them backward to get to the bus stop. I had to get home before Amy got home from school. Sighing, I straightened the backpack on my shoulders, which were rather sore, and walked toward the bus stop. There was no mistaking that this was the right house. Stopping at the base of the driveway, I noticed that the house was nothing to be intimidated by. It was just average; white with black shutters, not too big, a couple of toys scattered in the yard. Somehow seeing all this made me feel better and I walked a little faster to the front door. I ran inside, hoping Amy wasn't home yet. There was nothing, no sounds what so ever. I looked at the clock. I still had an hour before she returned. I had made it home in plenty of time. My shoulders slumped as I considered what to do next. There were some chairs on the front porch. Setting my backpack on the ground, I rolled my head from side to side to try to loosen the knots that had formed on my shoulders, then sat on one of the chairs. It felt good to sit after the long walk I had been on. I frowned and stared out at the street. No one seemed to be around.

Just then Ann appeared at the porch. "Hey, how are you?" I didn't want to talk to her at all, but she walked up on the porch and sat down.

"I am fine and how are you?" I said.

She asked me where my mother and father were. I didn't know what to say so I just told her he was at work and Mom went to the store. I knew she knew I was lying because Mom's car was gone and so was David's. It had been gone for days now. "You take care of yourself now," she said, before turning away and walking toward her house next door. I walked out to the backyard, closing the gate behind me, then went to the front porch and grabbed my backpack. Staring at the front door, wishing someone would help me, I felt despair enveloping me like mist on a foggy day. Why didn't I just tell her the truth and get her to help us? I was scared that they would separate Amy and I. I couldn't handle that.

Renewed hope pierced the cloud of despair like a beam of sunlight burning through the morning fog. Tossing my backpack over one shoulder, I stepped off the porch and marched toward the house next door. Not letting myself worry about what Ann would think of my wacky story, I pressed the doorbell and heard it pealing in the entry.

"Hi," I said lamely. She raised her eyebrows, obviously waiting for me to continue. "I, well, you asked if everything is okay, and, well, it's not."

"Oh, I see." I could feel my face crumpling and hot tears pushing their way into my eyes. She must have realized I was about to fall apart because she said, "Why don't you come in and tell me about it?"

I just nodded, my chin wobbly, and followed her inside. She closed the door behind me. I bit my lower lip, trying to control my emotions. She pointed to her living room. "Come sit down, why don't you?"

I did as she suggested, taking off my backpack before letting the soft chair embrace me. Ann sat across from me in a chair that was a twin to mine. How was I going to explain this?

"Can I get you something to drink?" She pushed herself out of her chair and stood.

"Okay, sure." I barely paid attention as she left the living room, but a moment later I faintly heard the sound of someone talking. Curious, I crept out of the living room and into a hallway. The voice became slightly louder as I silently made my way forward. As I moved down the hall, I glanced into a neighboring room and saw a desk with a large computer monitor on it. Sitting in the chair was my mom. I couldn't believe she was there. What was she doing there? I had told Ann she was gone and all the time she was over here. Alarm bells rang in my head and I knew I had to get out of there. Now.

Fat tears welled up in my eyes and slid down my cheeks. I felt completely alone. I was completely alone. I allowed myself to have a good cry, but after a while I was able to get my emotions under control. I wiped my face with the heels of my hands and stared into the distance, not thinking about anything in particular. I could see a few people shooting hoops on one of the basketball courts and others pushing children on swings in a play area, but no one was near me. Worn out, I took my jacket out of my backpack and sat on the porch while waiting on Amy to come home. A while later, I woke abruptly to the feeling of someone trying to tug my backpack out of my arms. I opened my eyes and saw Amy. She was smiling real big so I knew she had a wonderful day. I asked her if she was hungry because I had brought something home for her. I got the bag out of my backpack and handed to her. Her face lit up like it was Christmas time. "It's just a veggie burger, Amy," I said.

She said, "I know, but you saved it for me and that means you were thinking of me today. Has mom come home yet?" She asked. I told her she was next door and should be home soon.

We went inside to watch television for a while until Mom came home. All I could think about was if Ann told Mom I was there or not. Would she be mad at me when she did come home? I couldn't understand why she was at Ann's house in the first place. Why did Ann ask me where my mom was if she knew she was at her house? I was so confused. What was going on? Mom walked in the door and told Amy to go to bed and that she had to talk to me. *Oh God, here it comes.* Ann told her and now I was going to get it. She came and sat beside me. I looked at her face, trying to see if she was angry. At first, I couldn't tell but when she grabbed my arm, I knew she was mad. "What the hell were you doing at my job today?" She yelled.

Oh god, that woman told her I was there. "I was getting worried about you so I went looking for you," I said.

"Let me tell you, Girl, you don't come looking for me at all. How did you know I worked there"? She said.

"I remembered you telling me that you danced for money before, so I asked a waitress if she knew of any place like that," I replied.

"I have to have money for things that I need, so, yes, I do dance there, but that is none of your damn business and if I ever catch you sneaking around trying to find out shit like your grandma did, I will beat the shit out of you. Do you hear me?" She yelled.

I started to cry and all I could do was shake my head at her. She didn't like it when I didn't answer, but I was crying so hard I couldn't talk. The next thing I felt was the sting of her hand on my face. "Answer me, damn it!" she screamed.

"Yes, Mom, I understand!" I yelled back.

Chapter Twelve

The beginning of the end

The loud banging seemed to vibrate through my body. But maybe it was just my body shaking in terror at being in trouble again with Mom. I ran to the living room to see what was going on. It was only 5:00am so I couldn't figure out why someone would be making all that noise. What I saw shocked me. Mom was on the floor, beating it with a hammer. I didn't know whether to speak or not. She looked up at me with such anger in her eyes.

"Mom, are you okay?" I asked.

She didn't reply. She just sat there hitting the floor with the hammer over and over again. I didn't want to take the chance of her hitting me with it so I went back to my room and locked the door. Amy never woke up and that was a good thing. The pounding continued for a long time and finally it stopped. I walked down the hallway to see if she was still there, but the living room was empty with a huge hole in the floor. I snuck over to my mom's room and peeked in. She was lying across the bed, passed out. I went back to the room to get

Amy ready for school and myself as well. I had to go today; I had missed way too much.

***

The day seemed to drag on forever! All I wanted to do was go home and spend time with Amy. Finally, the last bell rang and we loaded the buses. As I got home and walked through the door, I yelled to see if Mom was home. She yelled that she was in the kitchen cooking dinner. That surprised me! I went to my room to put all my stuff away. Amy came through the door about ten minutes after I did. She had another great day at school by the smile on her face.

"Kelly, Amy, dinner's ready," Mom called up the hallway.

My stomach growled and I realized I was starving. As I went down the hallway, I tried to place the smell coming from the kitchen. When I entered the kitchen, I saw Mom moving pieces of cooked meat onto a plate.

"What is that?" I asked as I headed to the table, eager to satisfy my appetite.

"Liver," Mom said. I had begun pulling out a chair, but froze, not sure if I'd heard her right. It had sounded like she'd said liver, but she had said it like she would have said steak, or hamburgers, like it was a normal thing for us to eat.

"What?" I asked, hoping I had misunderstood.

"Liver," she repeated, a smile on her face.

Fortunately, she didn't notice me trying to withhold a gag. I sat in my chair and looked at the other items on the table, hoping I could fill up on the rolls and salad. A few moments later, we were all sitting at the table.

Mom began passing the food around. When the liver came to me, I passed it straight to Amy. "Kelly, what's wrong? Why aren't you taking any? You always eat my liver."

I like this stuff? I thought, trying to come up with an excuse for not eating it now. "Uh, we, that is, the school just had liver for lunch."

"Oh, I'm sorry. But you'd better have some anyway or you'll be hungry later."

"I thought I could just eat some extra rolls."

"Oh, Kelly. You know you only get one roll," Mom said, frowning.

"I do? How come?"

Her face reddened. "Maybe the school can afford to let their children have more than one roll each, but we, well, we just can't."

I didn't know why she was getting so upset all of a sudden, but I grabbed the plate of liver back from Amy and jabbed my fork into a small piece before dropping it on my plate. Then I noticed that Amy and she were staring at me.

"What?" I asked, annoyed. I managed to eat most of my serving of liver, but eventually I couldn't force down another bite. Not because I was full. In fact, I was still pretty hungry. But because after the first few bites, the texture and flavor made me want to vomit and I couldn't force myself to eat any more. Focusing on my one roll and my small serving of salad, I managed to eat enough to keep me going for a while. I thought that would have to do until morning, but then Mom announced she had something for dessert. Remembering the delicious desserts Grandma always made, I pictured a lovely slice of chocolate cake or a warm slice of apple pie. So when she brought out bowls of sliced bananas and poured milk into them, my anticipation quickly turned to disappointment. Hiding my displeasure at the lack of a sweet dessert, I took the bowl Mom handed me and ate all the bananas. No one seemed to notice anything out of the ordinary with me—at least no one said anything—so I finished my meal and carried my bowl over to the sink

When everyone was done, I started on the dishes, happy to have the solitude so I didn't have to pretend everything was normal. No one bothered me as I washed each dish by hand then dried them one by one. As I worked, my thoughts bounced between self-pity that I'd found myself in this predicament, and worry that I wouldn't be able to have a good life. After I put the last clean dish away, I headed to my room. I rested on my bed and thought about the world I lived in now. Everything was definitely different and I didn't much like it, but it seemed I didn't have a choice in the matter. It was so much different from living with Grandma. It was all too much for me to take in. Rolling over, I curled into a ball, wishing with all of my heart that I was just having a nightmare. I thought about the many times I'd had a bad dream and woken to realize it was all in my head and the utter relief I'd felt when I could think about the bad dream with detachment, because the horrible event in that dream hadn't actually happened. I never knew what to expect of my mother from one second to the next. It ws like the dreams. I never knew what they will be. Now I knew the exact opposite feeling. This was all too real and I couldn't escape it merely by waking up. This world was my new reality and I was scared.

***

I must have fallen asleep, because the next thing I knew Amy was shaking me and telling me it was time to get up. At first, I wondered why she was in my room, but then it all came back to me and I had fallen asleep early last night. It was time for school already. Forcing myself to get out of bed, I made my way to the bathroom and showered, then dug through the closet trying to find a pair of jeans that looked decent. Since there didn't seem to be anything I could do about my situation right now, I forced down the utter feeling of despair and made the best out of the day.

I went into the house and noticed how quiet it was and wondered where mom was. Not sure what to do, I pushed aside my concern and went into the kitchen to find a snack. Grandma usually had something for us to eat when we got home from school. Of course that was in my other life. In this new life who knew what the deal was with snacks. Food was such a major issue for everyone, for all I knew Mom would never make us snacks. I certainly didn't like that idea. I explored the contents of the cupboard, but didn't find anything that sounded good. "This really sucks," I muttered, craving one of my grandma's homemade chocolate chip cookies. "Wait a minute," I said, an idea occurring to me. Maybe I could make my own treats. Then I thought about Mom getting mad at me for making messes.

I grinned with a feeling of rebellion as I found flour, salt, baking soda, butter, eggs, and even some sugar, which surprised me. There were no chocolate chips, which didn't surprise me. I wondered how long I would have the house to myself, but had made enough batches of cookie dough to know I could do it in less than fifteen minutes. Having something normal to do made me feel really good. Almost like I was myself again. I started singing a song, a song that had been popular when Grandma and I baked together. Before long, I had finished making a batch of chocolate chip cookie dough, minus the chocolate chips. Scooping some up with a finger, I put it in my mouth and savored the sweet flavor. Even without the chocolate chips, it tasted wonderful. Then I filled a cookie sheet with small lumps of dough and placed it in the oven. When the first batch was done and cooled, I ate several cookies before drinking a glass of milk. As I was taking the second batch out of the oven, Amy walked in the door.

"What's that smell?" Amy asked as she walked into the kitchen.

"I made cookies," I squealed.

"Can I have one, Kelly?"

"Of course," I said as I handed her a cooled cookie.

She took a bite, then quickly ate the whole thing. "Can I have another?" she asked, her mouth full. I laughed and handed her another. Then Amy took another one.

"Well?" I asked as she chewed. "Do you like them?"

"They're delicious," Amy said. "I don't know if I've ever tasted something so good."

I smiled at her praise, but realized that she had. Grandma's cookies.

Mom never came home and we were left alone again. As we got ready for bed, I was thinking of a way for Amy and me to leave and never come back. I didn't know who would take care of us, but there had to be some nice people out there somewhere. I was sitting on my bed when I heard Amy screaming from the hallway. I ran as fast as I could to see what was wrong. There were flames everywhere. The kitchen was on fire and had made its way into the living room. I grabbed Amy and ran out the door. We ran next door to call the fire department. By the time they got there almost the entire house was burnt. I didn't know what we were going to do now. Ann asked me where my mother was and I told her at work. She had to work nights now. She looked at me with concern in her eyes. The firemen said it had started in the kitchen.

Oh god, I forgot to turn the oven off. It's all my fault that our house burnt to the ground. Mom was going to kill me for sure this time. Ann let Amy and I stay at her house for the night because she couldn't get hold of Mom.

As she took us to the room where we would sleep, she asked me a few questions that I really didn't want to answer but I did. "Does your mom stay gone a lot, Kelly?" she said. I answered with a nod. "Does your mom have a drug problem?" I really didn't want to answer that one, but I did with a nod. "

"Okay, Kelly, we will work all this out in the next couple of days."

I couldn't sleep at all that night. I was so scared of what was going to happen now. What if they came and take us away and separate Amy and me? I started to cry and Amy rolled over and hugged me tight and said, "It will be okay, Sissy. I promise."

***

The next morning I left the house and began walking to the school bus stop, dreading having to go to school today, but Ann said we had to. Thirty minutes later, I was at the school. I thought to myself I will make this a good day. I smiled, hoping that my luck would hold out and I would have a good day. Heading straight to my locker, I entered the combination, then looked at the books inside. I reluctantly pulled out the ones I would need for my first two classes, then closed the door and spun the lock. As I waited for the teacher to begin class, I pulled out my notebook and prepared to take notes. Even if I refused to be drawn into the fixation with being here I still had to face my mother, which meant I better have a good day now.

"Hi," the girl in front of me said, her body swiveled in my direction. "I'm Lori."

"I'm Kelly," I said, smiling at the friendly look on her face.

"I set a goal to talk to at least one new person each day. I've heard there are no strangers, just future friends."

"Oh. Well, that's a nice idea."

"I think so, too. That's why I've adopted it as my motto." Lori paused, but only for a second. "So, how long have you lived here? I don't think I've seen you around."

"My family just moved here a couple of months ago."

She nodded. "Do you like to run?"

I flashed back to a few days before when I'd chased after Amy, who had stolen my backpack. "Not really."

"That's too bad."

"Why's that?" I wasn't able to think of a single reason not running could be a bad thing. The teacher stood in front of the class then and everyone began to settle down.

"Because we need one more person on our relay track team," Lori whispered, before turning to face the front of the room. *Whatever*, I thought. When the teacher began her lecture, I tried to pay attention since I knew I had to catch up on my schoolwork. When class was over, Lori was right behind me as I left the classroom. "What class do you have next, Kelly?" she asked.

"English," I said, happy to have someone to walk with. "What about you?"

"My favorite class. Gym."

I never particularly liked gym, especially the part where I got all sweaty. "Why is it your favorite?"

"I just like to be active. That's why I run track."

"Oh. That's cool." But it still wasn't

something I saw myself doing by choice, although I knew I needed to decide about what sport I was going to do.

"Hey, Lori," a deep voice said from behind us. We both turned around.

"Hi, Connor," Lori said. I smiled at him, but didn't say anything. Today he looked even hotter than he had the day before. The blue of his shirt really set off his tanned face. "This is Kelly," Lori said. He smiled at me and I felt my heart flutter. I really never thought of boys before, but today that was all I could think about. "I tried to get her to join the track team," Lori said. "But she doesn't like to run."

"You don't like to run?" he asked, clearly shocked by such an idea.

"Well, I can do it," I said. "I just haven't done a lot of it lately." Suddenly, running was something I thought I might want to do more of.

"Then this is a good time to start," he said, an encouraging smile on his face. "Unless you already chose your sport?"

"Actually, no. I haven't." But now I knew what I was going to choose.

"Are you going to join track?" he asked.

"Sure. I mean, I guess so. I just need to let the office know, I guess."

"Okay. We'll tell the coach you'll be there for Monday's practice," Connor said.

Lori nodded, apparently not caring why I had suddenly changed my mind.

"Great," I said. "I'll see you guys there."

By the time lunch rolled around, I knew I would have plenty of homework, which would make my teacher happy that I was going to get caught up with everything.

***

At the end of school, I stopped by the office to report that I had chosen track as my sport. The woman behind the counter smiled in apparent approval and entered the information into the computer. Once that was done, I began the walkout when the lady asked me to wait a minute. I didn't know what was going on, but I sat on the bench beside the door.

Two women came out of the office and asked me if they could talk to me. I told them sure, but I didn't know what they wanted from me. They took me in a small room and started asking me all kinds of questions and the one lady kept saying,

"You can tell us the truth; we are here to help you."
They asked about my mother and why she was
gone so much and they asked me if I was being
abused by her. I answered every question with the
truth.

"Oh God! Amy, where is my sister Amy!" I
yelled.

"She is safe and you will see her soon." I
asked the woman where my mother was now. She
didn't know where she was; they had been trying
to track her down all day.

I even told her about the time my mother's
boyfriend touched me. When I started talking, it
was like I couldn't stop. I told her everything I saw
and everything I went through. She told me that
Amy and I were going to be placed in state custody
until they could find our mother and get this into
court. I didn't know what all that meant, but I did
know that my mother was in big trouble. She led
me out to her car and we went to get Amy. I was
scared, but at the same time I was relieved. It
seemed like we drove for hours before we finally
pulled up to this big building with lots of windows.
The elevator opened into a large foyer with
maroon walls and white pillars. The low ceiling and
dim recessed lighting gave the room a creepy yet
elegant vibe. There were chairs lined up against the
walls like a doctor's office. Was this a doctor's

office? I asked Mrs. Hollow if it was and she replied, "Yes, Sweetheart; we have to have you girls checked out by the doctor to make sure you are okay."

We locked eyes immediately, and as she approached I couldn't help but notice the change in atmosphere. Amy looked so scared and I could tell she had been crying. I ran up to her and held her tight and told her everything will be okay. I promised. She told me that the doctor looked at her everywhere and she was scared. I told her that they had to make sure that we were okay. She looked at me and said, "Now what do we do?" I told her what the woman told me and that we would be together until all this was worked out. I wanted to believe everything they were telling us, but a part of me was scared that they were lying. It was my turn to see the doctor so I followed the nurse back to a small room. First, he had me draw a picture of my mom's boyfriend who touched me. I drew two pictures of him, one of a man who was smiling and looked kind. The other was of a man with a devil-like look on his face, complete with horns and a tail. He then asked me a lot of questions, which I answered honestly.

He said in many families, when abuse comes to light, after parents recover from their shock and self-blame, they consult with professionals and do whatever they must in order to deal with the effects on their children and themselves and ensure that it never happens again. Blame! "My mother blames me for this, not herself," I told him. She left with him after this happened and didn't return for a few days. She hit me for this, not him. She hated me for what he done to me. I couldn't help but start to cry. He told me that it was almost over and then I could go be with my sister. The exam seemed to go on forever. He checked me everywhere and I was so embarrassed by all of it. I wanted to climb in a hole and bury myself. Why did we have to go through this? Why couldn't our mother love us enough to give all her habits up?

Epilogue

A new Beginning

20 years later

"Doctor Green, you have a phone call," the nurse said as she stuck her head in the door of the exam room.

"Who is it, Melody?" I asked.

"It's your grandmother" she said.

"Tell her I will call her back in just a few minutes," I replied.

Yes, my mother had lied about a lot of things when I was a child and one of them was that my grandmother had died. After Amy and I left that doctor's office that day, we were not taken to a place we didn't know. We were taken to our Grandmother's house to live with her until the court date came up. It was the happiest day of our lives. We were home once again in the loving arms of our grandmother. It took the courts months to convict my mother of neglect and child abuse, but once they did the judge gave my grandmother full custody of Amy and me. My mother served two years in jail and when she got out, she moved out of state and we never heard from her again. We grew up with the love and caring that we always wanted and needed. Amy graduated High school and went to college to be a lawyer. For me, I wanted to be like my grandmother and help other people get well, so I went into the medical field and became a doctor. My grandmother always told me that we chose our lives and how they turned out. Well, Amy and I chose to go down a better path and have what we never had with our mother. Amy had a wonderful husband and two beautiful children who adored her. I had a wonderful husband and three children who adored *me*. My grandmother was still alive and well, and spending each day with her great grandchildren, who looked up to her in a very special way.

Children who have parents with drug addiction should know that if something ever happens to you that you know is wrong you have the right to speak out. There are many people who would help you. You never have to face this alone. Abuse is not your fault and you should never feel ashamed because it is the reasonability of the parent to keep you safe, not harm you, I wrote in the notebook that I had been using to gather my notes and experiences in order to write a tell-all novel for others suffering from abuse and neglect.

These are the statewide abuse
hotline numbers! If you know any
child who is being abused or
molested, please call and get
them help.

Alabama

(800-422-4453) for assistance.

Alaska

Toll-Free:(800) 478-4444

Arizona

Toll-Free:(888) SOS-CHILD (888-767-2445)

Arkansas

Toll-Free:(800) 482-5964

Colorado

Local (toll):(303) 866-5932

Connecticut

TDD:(800) 624-5518

Toll-Free:(800) 842-2288

Delaware

Toll-Free:(800) 292-9582

District of Columbia

Local (toll):(202) 671-SAFE (202-671-7233)

Florida

Toll-Free:(800) 96-ABUSE (800-962-2873)

Georgia

(800-422-4453) for assistance.

Hawaii

Local (toll):(808) 832-5300

Idaho

TDD:(208) 332-7205

Toll-Free:(800) 926-2588

Illinois

Toll-Free:(800) 252-2873

Local (toll):(217) 524-2606

Indiana

Toll-Free:(800) 800-5556

Iowa

Toll-Free:(800) 362-2178

Kansas

Toll-Free:(800) 922-5332

Kentucky

Toll-Free:(877) 597-2331

Louisiana

Toll-Free:(855) 452-5437

Maine

TTY:(800) 963-9490

Toll-Free:(800) 452-1999

Maryland

(800-422-4453) for assistance.

Massachusetts

Toll-Free:(800) 792-5200

Michigan

Fax:(616) 977-1154

(616) 977-1158

Toll-Free:(855) 444-3911

Minnesota

® (800-422-4453) for assistance.

Mississippi

Toll-Free:(800) 222-8000

Local (toll):(601) 359-4991

Missouri

Toll-Free:(800) 392-3738

Montana

Toll-Free:(866) 820-5437

Nebraska

Toll-Free:(800) 652-1999

Nevada

Toll-Free:(800) 992-5757

New Hampshire

Toll-Free:(800) 894-5533

Local (toll):(603) 271-6556

New Jersey

TDD:(800) 835-5510

TTY:(800) 835-5510

Toll-Free:(877) 652-2873

New Mexico

Toll-Free:(855) 333-7233

New York

TDD:(800) 369-2437

Toll-Free:(800) 342-3720

Local (toll):(518) 474-8740

North Carolina

(800-422-4453) for assistance.

North Dakota

(800-422-4453) for assistance.

Ohio

Toll-Free:(855) 642-4453

Oklahoma

Toll-Free:(800) 522-3511

Oregon

(800-422-4453) for assistance.

Pennsylvania

TDD:(866) 872-1677

Toll-Free:(800) 932-0313

Puerto Rico

Toll-Free:(800) 981-8333

Local (toll):(787) 749-1333

Rhode Island

Toll-Free:(800) RI-CHILD (800-742-4453)

South Carolina

Local (toll):(803) 898-7318

(800-422-4453) for assistance.

South Dakota

(800-422-4453) for assistance.

Tennessee

Toll-Free:(877) 237-0004

Texas

Department of Family and Protective Services

Toll-Free:(800) 252-5400

Utah

Toll-Free:(855) 323-3237

Vermont

After hours:(800) 649-5285

Virginia

Toll-Free:(800) 552-7096

Local (toll):(804) 786-8536

Washington

TTY:(800) 624-6186

Toll-Free:(800) 562-5624

 (866) END-HARM (866-363-4276)

West Virginia

Toll-Free:(800) 352-6513

Wisconsin

(800-422-4453) for assistance.

Wyoming

(800-422-4453) for assistance.

Always remember a child's life is precious!

Drug – Abuse hotline: http://beta.samhsa.gov/find-help/national-helpline

Dedications:

I want to dedicate this book to all the children who have or had a parent of addiction. Stay strong and never give up hope!

Our lives can change in a split second from good to bad and from bad to good. We must just keep believing and always have hope for a new day!

Acknowledgements:

First, I want to thank my family for encouraging me to continue to write.

To my editor and publisher Genevieve Scholl, I wouldn't know what to do without you.

To all my Facebook friends, of whom there are too many to name, but you know who you are! I love each and every one of you. Without your support, I wouldn't be here right now.

And finally, to all my indie author friends, you have given me the strength to keep going on this journey of mine.

About the author:

I am an indie author! I live in West Virginia. I am a single mother of five children. I started writing for fun when I was younger and decided to go further with it. This journey has been a wonderful experience. I am so excited about my new book. I hope everyone enjoys it! I find that everyday life can be such an inspiration for writing. I love writing about everyday experiences. I also want to write about romance in the near future. My next book will be a YA book and I hope to get into a lot of other genres.

You can find me at:

http://www.amazon.com/Outside-Addiction-Mothers-Sandra-Shrewsbury-ebook/dp/B00ERYQ5RM/ref=la_B00ES3VPXG_1_1?s=books&ie=UTF8&qid=1409549646&sr=1-1

https://www.facebook.com/sandra.shrewsbury

https://www.facebook.com/SandraShrewsbury.Author?ref=hl

Printed in Great Britain
by Amazon.co.uk, Ltd.,
Marston Gate.